good deed rain

Books by Allen Frost

Ohio Trio
Bowl of Water
Another Life
Home Recordings
The Mermaid Translation
The Selected Correspondence of Kenneth Patchen
The Wonderful Stupid Man
Saint Lemonade
Playground
Roosevelt
5 Novels
The Sylvan Moore Show
Town in a Cloud
A Flutter of Birds Passing Through Heaven:
A Tribute to Robert Sund
At the Edge of America
Lake Erie Submarine
The Book of Ticks
I Can Only Imagine
The Orphanage of Abandoned Teenagers
Different Planet
Go with the Flow: A Tribute to Clyde Sanborn
Homeless Sutra
The Lake Walker
A Hundred Dreams Ago
Almost Animals
The Robotic Age
Kennedy

Kennedy ©2018
Allen Frost, Good Deed Rain
Bellingham, Washington
ISBN 978-1-64370-399-2

Cover & Illustrations: Fred Sodt
Writing: Allen Frost
Apple: TFK!
Thanks to Larry Smith & Helen Frost for comments

This book is for Fred

Credits:
　　Robert F. Kennedy quote from *Bobby Kennedy: The Making of a Folk Hero* by Lester David; Dodd, Mead, New York, 1986.
　　Wallace Stevens quote from *Letters of Wallace Stevens*, edited by Holly Stevens; A.A. Knopf, New York, 1966.
　　Bob Kaufman poem excerpted from *The Ancient Rain*; New Directions, New York, 1981.
　　Route 66, "Love is a Skinny Kid," CBS television Season 2, episode 25, aired April 6, 1962.
　　John F. Kennedy speeches:
　　"For the opening of the World's Fair in Seattle," April 21, 1962.
　　"Cuban Missile Crisis" delivered on radio at 4 PM West Coast Time, October 22, 1962.

Allen Frost

"I found out something I never knew. I found out that my world was not the real world."

—Robert F. Kennedy

"I believe that with a bucket of sand and a wishing lamp I could create a world in half a second that would make this one look like a hunk of mud."

—Wallace Stevens

All those flowers that you never grew—
    that you wanted to grow
The ones that were plowed under
    ground in the mud—
Today I bring them back
And let you grow them
Forever.

—Bob Kaufman

Asleep
Waiting
School
Caroline
Rockets
Hickory Road
Cigarettes
Frogs
Pumpkins
Cape Canaveral
Things to Say
Flying Saucer
Apples
The Stand
Starlight
Lucky
Evaporating
Milkman
Meteor
Candlelight
Nowhere
Dinosaurs
Speed
War
Bayview
Angel Eyes
Moonlite
Masks
Sunshine
Poetry
Fossils
Lobster
Daylong
Fugitives
Meaning

Testing
Constellation
What To Say
Floating
Splash
Numbers
Armor
Better
Pretend
Forces
Stories
Movies
Salmon
Vision
Shock
Alone
The Path
Birds
Dowsing
Still Around
Coal
Spellbound
Treasure
Daydream
Pages
Ghost
Shovel
Moonlight
Caught
Kitchen
Kennedys
Stones
Realities
Rolling
Song

Relief
Space
Gunshot
Tipped
Cafeteria
Ice Cream
Soon
Practice
Courage
Rain
Maybe
The World's Smallest Island
Knowing
Windblown
Legend
Secrets
Futuristic
Good Night

FRIDAY, October 12, 1962

ASLEEP

It rained during the night. A soft weeping brushed the roof as Avery lay awake staring at the slanted ceiling, listening. That sound was the end of summer. It meant the blue sky was remembering how to rain, and the cold, wet days and nights of winter weren't far away. Unable to sleep, he cast his mind out.

From his little upstairs room in the eaves, he sailed out over the apple trees, around the poplars, the roadside stand with its Tweed Farm sign, and he landed, gaining speed on Donovan Ave, using it as a runway to take off with a rush of speed. He was above the trees and farms of the valley cut into patchwork by fences and streams and one-lane dirt roads. Avery turned his head to look past his shoulder to the south and he could see that new highway inching its way closer to their town. It cut a long moon white path, unrolling a hundred miles through all the green, right between the houses of towns, crossing rivers and blasted hillsides, all the way to Seattle and then going on further to Oregon and California. At night, when he couldn't sleep, Avery thought of that highway getting closer every day and he thought of all the cars and trucks on it tipped and waiting to rush forward. With his thoughts somewhere out there, with the last days of summer turned into hushing rain on the roof, Avery fell back asleep. School had started again. It wouldn't be long before he had to get up.

WAITING

By morning, the sky had turned to a beautiful blue and the sun coming up colored the clouds pink. A mist clung to the tops of the trees and blanketed the Chuckanut Hills. Little birds were singing in the leaves and high up a string of seagulls went by, looking down for food.

Avery left his driveway and his shoes crunched on the gravel shoulder of Donovan. A steep drop-off into the ditch ran alongside the road. Down through the tall weeds and clover, a trickle of water flowed. He could hear the crackly stream in the places where it dropped over stones. When he was younger, Avery would come here to make dams and watch the water thicken into wider pools and even overflow on the road. He could also hear another sound this early morning. The machinery was already at work on the highway. It made a low rumble and clank like the engine room of a ferryboat.

Avery stopped at a worn spot where he had kicked the gravel clear, a little scuffed circle of ground where he waited for the bus. He admired that sky again and turned his eyes to the clear view of the creek. This had been his spot and view since he started taking the bus in grade school.

When the ditch was full of water as it was on this October day, he could stare into that reedy water and imagine little worlds of mermaids and submarines. Once he thought he saw a salmon, flashing silver, but his father assured him that was impossible. It must have been a bit of tinfoil, or the flash off a broken bottle. And even though his father laughed and shook his head, Avery returned that evening to the spot with his bamboo pole to stand there dipping a lure for an hour before returning home. After all the years, he looked at that thin stream and waited to see the salmon reappear.

SCHOOL

The yellow school bus came slowly from the top of Donovan. It hid for a moment behind the big rock in the middle of the road. Left from the last glacial age, the Donovan Rock loomed there so big the road had to split to go around it.

The bus reappeared like a goldfish. Avery took one last look at the stream.

He held his geometry book, American history, and a notebook binder.

Across the road from Avery, an old horse stood in a thicket of young alder. Avery waved to him—that was General—a horse rumored to be a hundred years old. General's ears twitched as the bus approached. The ancient horse looked the other way as the bus hissed and braked to where Avery waited.

When the wide yellow door flipped open, Avery stepped on board.

"Good morning, Avery," said the driver.

"Hello."

The driver let him find a seat halfway up the aisle before he started the bus moving again.

The bus followed the road through the orchards, farms and fields. It passed the gray boat hull left on a lawn. Once used for crabbing out in the bay, it had been pulled ashore and now it lay, slowly splitting apart on a bed of damp grass and dandelions. Someone painted PT-109 on it, just like the song on the radio. Then the bus began to climb the hill out of all that green. They passed the house by the pond where Avery's grandparents lived. From the top of the hill was a view of the town, houses, a couple church steeples, a cluster of old brick buildings that formed the downtown, the pharmacy, bars and a hardware store. The road drove right to the end of land, the cannery and shipyard sitting by the bay all aglow with the new sunshine.

The bus—crowded with the sound of talking, laughing, bursts of song—passed the fire station with its red engine sitting gleaming outside and turned left on Finnegan Way at the corner of the IGA.

A newsprint photo of Marilyn Monroe was passed hand to hand over Avery. Since her death a couple months ago, her pictures were everywhere. There was a hoot from the back of the bus as the picture made it there. Avery thought about Marilyn Monroe. It was hard not to, as the bus crossed the bridge over Padden Creek. It seemed to float high above the water, a hundred feet below, shining with rapids in the lush green brush. Ahead of them was the high school.

Even though the morning light reflected on its walls, white against a blue sky, with the tall flagpole above it like a big ocean steamer, Avery caught sight of it and groaned. Oh no, he thought, and they were all headed straight for it, like that island in Pinocchio. Then, as the bus crawled around the turn on Hawthorne Road and he could see everyone else getting off buses or milling around the sidewalk, strolling or hurrying up the stairs in bounds, he remembered Caroline.

She was there somewhere. And suddenly the school really was a big ocean steamer with Caroline on deck or down one of those halls and he would wait all day just to catch sight of her. He would too—between classes, the hallways filled with the noisy pour and push of traffic—he would search past every shoulder and arm looking for Caroline. There were only a few minutes before the next bell rang and everyone better be in their classroom. That was all he hoped for. If she happened to be there walking with a friend, or shutting her locker on the second floor, time was captured and she was cupped in his memory.

The bus stopped with a lurch and a pneumatic hiss and everyone piled down the aisle, still talking and laughing and singing Chubby Checker off key. Avery waited until Ted Jacobs waddled past, then he stood up and followed. Another school day had begun.

CAROLINE

The sun came up, shined in the windows, swung on its slow path across the blue sky and Avery went from one class to the next, head bowed over book and writing assignments. He got a quiz back in history, marked 68 in red pen and he folded it into his notebook. The teacher's voice was like a radio reporting years and wars with bulletins written in squeaking chalk. Avery found himself starting to daydream. The yellow pencil drifted off course from words about the Colony and before he knew it, he had written Caroline. Her name had appeared so out of the blue it looked like someone had planted a flower in all those rows of lead colored words.

Avery put his thumb over her name and glanced to his left and right. Meryl Watson was busy writing. Stu Bausch had his eyes closed, hand to his head. Avery moved his thumb just enough to look again. Caroline's name was still there.

The long Friday at school was nearly over and he hadn't seen her. He had even been a minute late getting to history class, running from the floor where her locker was. Were they missing each other by seconds all day? He would appear in the hall just as she turned a corner? She went in a door as he came out another? Was it all as choreographed as a ballet on Dick Van Dyke's show? Saturday and Sunday would be two long days of waiting to see her on Monday. He considered writing her name again.

In cursive, her letters rolled along, watery as waves onto a beach. He started to draw little lines, sketching them softly about her. He drew a vine from the top of her *C*, to loop all around and connect with the *e* at the end of her name. He added flowers and a hummingbird like the ruby throat one that buzzed the fuchsia below the window back at home. He gave her name a whole garden and was starting to draw a rabbit when Stu snorted and held a hand over his grin.

"Is there a problem, boys?" Mr. Benson asked.

There was the chirping sound of chairs as everyone in the class turned in their seats.

Without looking at his notebook, Avery let his pencil scribble over her name. "No, sir," he said.

"Then you won't mind if I continue?"

Avery shook his head. There was a moment of laughter from the class and he knew he was blushing, bowing his head, covering the scratched out name with his hand.

"In 1620, the Mayflower landed in Cape Cod, Massachusetts."

Oh no! Avery almost said out loud. Somehow a hundred years had passed him by while he was writing Caroline. No wonder he got a 68 on the last quiz. It was so easy to lose track of years, but somewhere in time, between the fall of the Aztecs and the Mayflower landing, there was Caroline.

ROCKETS

The bell rang and there was a flip of notebooks closing up and down all the rows. A pencil clattered on the floor and chairs were scooting back.

Stu Bausch gave Avery a sock on the arm. "Kook!" he laughed.

Avery shuffled into line with the rest of them. He watched the back of Kenny Breen's red and white checkered shirt as they all slipped out the door, into the hallway. He flowed right in with the crowd, stepped out of the stream as he reached his locker.

He spun the combination dial right, left, right and opened the bright orange door. Up on the top shelf he tossed his history book and shut the door with a hollow slam. Everyone was on their way outside and Avery joined in for those big double doors that all day held out the sun and the breeze, but at 3 o'clock were propped open to let them all out.

A long row of school buses were waiting with engines idling or starting up with a chuff of diesel.

Avery went down the steps and weaved through girls with headbands, sweaters and skirts, two boys who had a football and were throwing it overhead. He was almost to his bus when he saw Caroline. She was talking to a friend. He slowed down. His feet came to a halt all by themselves.

She wore a green jacket, bright green as the moss that tucked into the seams of 9th Street. There was a white barrette in her brown hair. She held a stack of books in front of her. Avery was bumped by someone running past to catch a bus that stopped and opened up its door. Avery was bent with the commotion like a sunflower that goes back and forth when knocked. Oh Caroline, he thought, and wished he had the guts just to walk past and say hello. He took a step forward as if he meant to do that, but something else stopped that from happening.

As the bus groaned forward beside him, someone slapped on the window. Avery looked. It was Ted Jacobs, face big as a jack o' lantern, waving at him.

Avery's bus ride home left the school, left him standing there smelling exhaust. He had this dream before. It wasn't that bad—he could walk home—as in his dreams, the world would transform around him as he went into some new thing.

While the bus got smaller, Avery turned towards the crosswalk so he could beeline over the wide lawn in front of the school, over to Hawthorne, Finnegan and Donovan back home. It only took a footstep though for him to look up from that sunny sidewalk and see Caroline headed his way. Her friend got on Bus 25 and she was all alone.

He didn't have much time, but he had been here in dreams. She was there, close as the rain on his ceiling last night, when he looked into her eyes and said, "Hello."

She smiled.

Avery looked away as they passed. He was careful not to step on her shadow, taking an extra step that he needed not to fall and he was almost floating. He felt he was walking on air: if his feet weren't plugged into his white sneakers he would have been drifting off into the branches, spinning away like a dandelion seed. I did it! That was so easy, he smiled.

He looked both ways and ran the crosswalk and hopped over the curb onto the grass. He squeezed his own hand. That was so easy to talk to her he could do it again. She actually smiled! He shut his eyes and he could see it happen. He only said a word and look what happened. Imagine that...

He opened his eyes and it was a good thing he did.

He jumped a little patch of daisies growing in a whorl. Sometimes on the farm he would pick those and string them together by their long stems to make a chain. But he never had anyone to give a necklace to before.

Avery left the soft lawn and stepped back onto concrete. Some other kids were waiting on the corner, Tony and Harold Evans. Harold punched the silver button on the post for the light to change.

"Hey Tweed," Tony said. "You still make those rockets?" The two of them shuffled, scratching the curb.

"I haven't made any rockets for a while."

The light changed to red and the three of them stepped into the road, following the traffic guard, an old man who wore a dark blue uniform and held an orange flag out at a slant for them. The old man walked with a limp and was nearly deaf, but Tony kept quiet until they made the opposite curb. Then he asked right away, "We need some rockets for tomorrow night. Can you make us some?"

Harold added, "We'll give you a dime apiece."

Tony fished in his pocket. "Here. Here's a dollar. Cash in advance."

Harold patted Avery on the back.

"I haven't made them for a while."

"Come on, Tweed!" Tony pressed the dollar into Avery's hand.

Avery said, "Maybe I can make a few."

"Ten," Tony said. "We need ten."

"That's the deal," said Harold.

"Oh, okay."

"Great!" Tony grinned. "Bring them to the freeway tomorrow night at seven."

"Alright..." Avery crumpled the dollar into his jeans. The two boys hurried off from him, down Cowgill Ave. They were laughing and happy. They got what they wanted. Avery wasn't that pleased though. He stopped making rockets after the last one he made blew up in his hand. It gave him a terrible scare. Anyway, he had something better to think about than rockets.

He rewound his memory like a fluid reel of film, to the school, minutes ago, to that smile that made his day. He could walk along by himself remembering that and he didn't feel alone at all. Her smile had set in motion everything around him—the gardens, the birds, the colors of houses, the hum of wires, radios and the warm clean smell of the laundromat.

HICKORY ROAD

Avery wasn't too far down Donovan when he heard a car horn behind him and as the long blue wood paneled station wagon slowed to a stop, his grandmother called him, "Yoohoo!" out the unrolled window.

He crossed the road and hurried around to the passenger side and got in.

"Hello, Avery," she reached over and squeezed his hand. "I was just out shopping for groceries. Did you miss your bus?"

"Sort of."

She put the car back into gear and they were rolling. Not too fast though. She never went over 25 on this road. Avery imagined that was horse and buggy high speed, as quick as she would ever want to go. He took a nervous look behind them. Sometimes cars would roar up on their bumper, especially those loud ones the high school seniors drove, and with a roar they would pass her station wagon, throwing gravel and cloud. She just couldn't believe other drivers like that. She kept both hands on the wheel and steered where she knew the next destination would be waiting.

They passed the familiar skyline of hills and trees. Avery saw an eagle way up near a cloud. There was a white plate of moon.

"Did you have a good day at school?"

He had a ready answer, but then he remembered and smiled, "Yes."

"Oh good." Her eyes were intent behind her gold glasses, watching the slow road. "I got some fish for supper, and green beans. I even bought some ice cream for your grandfather." She gave him a very quick look, "He's feeling better today."

Avery nodded. During the last year his grandfather

had been slowing down. On bad days he would stay in bed, coughing. On better days, Avery would stretch out beside him and they would watch *Perry Mason* and his grandfather would lie there with his hands folded over his chest and his breathing would be a ragged, steady cutting saw.

The car speed slowed by half. Avery watched the speedometer needle drop as she waited for Hickory Road. Avery was glad there wasn't a truck full of hay behind them.

The wheels dipped into the gravel and the long car slid along with a snowy sound. Their little dark wooden house was in some fir trees beside a pond on their right. She turned off the road after the mailbox. There was an old rusted anchor sloped in the weeds. It was a relic from Avery's grandfather's ocean days.

She parked next to a big patch of dried orange lilies and Avery pushed open the heavy car door. He reached back and got the paper grocery bag. He could see the carton of vanilla ice cream. The lid was dotted with melting crystals. He closed the door with his knee and followed his grandmother on that path that led to the house.

Their feet crunched on white bits of broken seashell. Every once in a while they would go down to the beach on Poe's Point and collect a bucket of more clam shells washed ashore. Strewn on the path, they almost glowed at night, crackling underfoot between the dark sigh of Douglas fir.

His grandmother in her blue flat sneakers, blue slacks and windbreaker, with her purse swinging from her hand, pointed at the birdfeeder where a squirrel hung from a coconut, head stuffed in the round hole to get at the sunflower seeds. "Would you look at that?" There were some chickadees on the flat feeder tray and a small red and black woodpecker tapping at the suet.

She opened the front door and went in, but Avery paused as he always did to ring the brass ship's bell attached to the frame. It made a bright clang that instantly made Avery think of the English Channel and a convoy in the fog.

"Warren!" his grandmother called, "We're home."

In the entry room, where big glass windows looked back up into the green towards the road where they parked, she took off her coat and hung it on a hook by the door. When Avery was younger, a few years ago, he used to build model airplanes on spread-out newspapers on the flat lid above the water pump. This was also where one summer night, a big luna moth flung itself across the glowing yellow glass, thumping like a hand. Avery kept his coat on and followed her into the kitchen.

He put the groceries on the counter beside the black transistor radio and at the other side of the kitchen, past the big oil stove, the bedroom door slid open on noisy rollers. The little sign on it, *Day Sleeper*, moved into the recess of the wall.

Avery's grandfather stood there, holding onto the edge of the door, looking thin in his baggy blue work clothes but he was standing and smiling and happy to see his wife and grandson. "Well..." he said slowly, "Good to see you, Avery. How was school?"

"Good." As he thought of Caroline again, he almost said, "Great!" but maybe he would tell them about that later.

The old man walked gingerly from the room and took his seat at the table by the window, with his back to the big white refrigerator. He yawned wide and loud.

"How was your nap, Warren?" Eileen asked. She carried the grocery bag to the sink and was unloading it, first putting the ice cream in the cold drawer at the top of the fridge.

Warren said, "I woke up just before you got home." By the habit of years, he reached into his shirt pocket and took out a crumpled packet of Marlboros. His hand trembled slightly as he held it.

"Remember, only one a day," Eileen said.

"I know, I know." He put the cigarettes back into his pocket, tucked behind his folded black rimmed glasses.

CIGARETTES

Time got lost for a while in their kitchen. These were things Avery took for granted then.

Eileen prepared their supper while Avery and Warren talked. A big silver kettle boiled on the stove, turned into cups of tea while Warren sipped at a can. Avery visited his grandparents nearly every day after school, sat at the table, listened to stories, had tea with milk and a couple cold gingersnaps and it was the sort of routine and good feeling that he never imagined being without. Only later on would he look back and know memories can live where you can't go anymore.

The window got darker and by the end of their meal it shined like a black sea stone. Around about that time, Warren would take out his cigarettes and pull one and sort of roll it gently between his fingers. He used to smoke a lot of them so now these slowed down motions built to the event like a ritual. He had a little boat ashtray, dory shaped, filled with the color and smell of ash. Eileen would get up to stand by the stove as if she had suddenly become very cold and Warren would fish in his shirt pocket for a book of matches.

His hands had done this hundreds of times but now they shook as he stuck the cigarette in his lips and tore free a paper match. Striking it, he brought the fire up and it trembled against the cigarette. He cupped his hands around it as if he was in the wind. His eyes narrowed to the heat and smoke as he drew and puffed out that first cloud.

Warren shook out the match and dropped it into the dory and he pulled the smoke into him and breathed it out.

Avery liked that first catch of fire and draw, he even liked the first smell of the lit cigarette and he liked the way the slightly blue smoke curled and disappeared in the air. But after it burned a little more, Avery would sit back a little further, out of the grab of the smell and smoke. And he didn't like the way his grandmother would stand away from them, busying herself with the hand towels or socks drying on the wooden rack that stood by the oil stove. She would always come back when that one cigarette was done, but Avery could tell she didn't like it a million times more than him.

Warren took as much from the cigarette as he could and then finally crushed it into the boat where tackle and folded nets should have been stowed. He coughed and took another sip from the tin can to cool off his throat. He pushed back his chair, took a look out the black window and only saw himself in the reflection.

"I guess I better get back home," Avery said. It was dark but he knew the way home would be lit by moonlight.

The smoke made him sleepy. His eyelids were heavy and his body felt heavy. He knew the cool night air would wake him up again.

FROGS

So Avery scooted his chair back and his grandmother kissed him and gave him two cookies to take on his walk and his grandfather stood up too.

"Thanks for the food." Avery pulled on his coat from off the back of the chair. He put one of the cookies in a pocket. He was thinking ahead—what if a coyote cornered him out on the dark path? He used to listen to a record album of *Peter and the Wolf* and it wasn't hard to imagine those songs playing as he crossed the little farm in the bumpy shadows of the apple trees and poplars.

His grandmother walked with him to the door and they said goodbye again and Avery took a step into the cool air and gave that bell another ring like he always did. She waved at him through the screen window and he hopped out onto the shells.

Instead of following the path back up to the road, he walked past the birdfeeder tree. Of course there were no birds at this hour, they were all sleeping somewhere hidden who knows where. The path took a steep plunge. He knew the way though, digging his heels as he approached the pond in their backyard. It was a mirror of moonlight. Summers ago he used to swim in there. His feet would stand and wriggle in the mud, soft as butter.

When he was ten, he spent a hot week in August trying to find a bullfrog that lived on the reedy shore. It always managed to hop away from him until his grandfather gave Avery a tip. When they were out on a walk, Warren pointed at the tall blue heron stepping cautiously up a stream. "See that Walky-Up-The- Creeky?" They stopped and he put a hand on Avery's shoulder. "How do you think he manages to catch his fill of frogs every day?"

Avery observed the bird and answered, "He walks real slow."

His grandfather nodded. "Mmhm. But that's not all. You can't tell from here, but if you could get up close, you would hear that bird making a sound, a high pitched hum just like a juicy fly. That's what really gets that frog. He can't help himself—he has to sneak out of the cover and next thing you know, it's all over." Warren stuck out his hand like a beak hitting water.

After that, Avery became that bird his grandfather described. Jeans rolled up over his knees, he took big slow wide steps in the mud, humming up high and even though he went all around the pond that way with the old man watching and smiling, he didn't catch a frog. Warren assured Avery when the boy came back ashore there wasn't a finer bird imitator. The frogs just weren't hungry that day.

Avery heard what must have been the great, great grandson of that original frog give a croak. It made him think of how foolish he must have looked—a boy trying to be a heron—but it was funny too, he knew.

He circled the pond's edge, by the sign his grandfather put up a long time ago: *No Fishing*. The joke was, there were no fish in there. Still, it hadn't stopped Avery from trying.

PUMPKINS

A blackberry caught his sleeve, but Avery pulled it free. There were places where the path squeezed in between the shrubs and vines and sumac. It probably wouldn't be long before the farm was overgrown. In truth, it wasn't much of a farm anymore. Avery's grandparents were old, Warren was sick. Avery's father and brother were gone and Avery had to spend most days in school while his mother had to work in town to make ends meet. Who was left to work the land? All they could do was pick some of the hundreds of ripe apples to make cider for a little roadside cash. The air was sweet and sour with the smell of the rest of the crop dropping from branches and rotting on the ground. How much longer did the farm have to live?

The frog gave him a single goodbye croak. Avery took it to be a sort of "no hard feelings" as he left the pond behind him, sparking with white light and a long line of frogs living there alone.

Up on the rim of the pond, out of the brambles, the land flattened out into a patchwork of fields. All the Tweed apple trees stood in rows in tall yellowing grass, throwing shadows on the bumpy weedy ground. Avery took a bite out of that cookie he'd been holding all this time, round in his hand like a skipping stone. He ate it in four bites. He could have reached out for one of the apples he walked by—the trees were full of them, branches dipped his way. Tomorrow he would help his grandparents make cider. He took their place now, turning the press.

He spotted an owl on a branch with a good view of the field, eyes clicking on the smallest movement of mice in the grass. Sometimes an owl would glide over Avery quietly as a rushing cloud. In his surprise, all he would see was a blur.

At the end of the property, Avery climbed the fence and dropped onto the soft soil of the next yard. This one was planted with rows of pumpkins. Swelled up like balloons, they looked like they had bubbled up from the ground, gleaming in the night, waiting for candles in them to blink on. Suddenly he remembered *The Invasion of the Body Snatchers* and the seed pods that grew like these, filled with the people you thought you knew. After it played on *The Count Misfit Show,* Avery hid in his bed in the midnight gloom and stared out the window, past the curtains at the black and white fields. How easy it would be to quietly grow a whole other town and replace everyone in the dead of night.

CAPE CANAVERAL

He hurried through the pumpkin crop and slid between a fencepost and an alder tree. This section of land was left overgrown, the stalks of grass made a deep gray lake he waded in. He saw the silhouette of General not far away. The old horse was watching him. Avery saluted. General managed to wander the whole valley regardless of fences or streams or bogs. Sometimes Avery wondered if the old horse could fly. The grass swished around him and Avery could see the peaked roof of his house and more apple trees in between.

There was a light left on the porch. It made an orange dot in the dark. He climbed the slats of cedar fence and straddled it as if he sat on a saddle. He looked back to wave goodnight to General but there was no sign of him. Sometimes General would go missing for days. He had a lot of territory.

Avery crawled down onto his side of the fence and ran the rest of the way, under the ripe apples, under the washing lines rigged with clean, damp laundry, the old chicken coop and the orange light on the porch grew to a glow that waved with moths. He jumped onto the wooden steps of home, grabbed the handrail and heaved himself up onto a loud landing on the porch. The pot of geraniums shook.

He could see the kitchen light on inside but his mother wouldn't be home yet. He turned the door handle and it opened with a creak. He still expected to see their dog waiting for him. His long nose would find his hand, his gold fur pushed against him in greeting. It made the house seem all the quieter and darker without that happy dog.

He let the door click shut behind him and he slipped off his muddy shoes. He didn't want his mother coming home from work to see the footprints of *The Creature from the Black Lagoon.*

The floorboards creaked as he walked into the kitchen. He still had some time to gather rocket supplies. He opened the drawer lowest to the floor by the sink and found a roll of silver tinfoil. He got two boxes of wooden matches, tape and skewers, a pair of scissors and a few little round flat candles. It wasn't Cape Canaveral, but with everything he needed, he carried the armful out of the kitchen and up the steep stairs to his bedroom.

THINGS TO SAY

Way up in the eaves of the house, sometimes he still bumped his head on the sloping ceiling. He had to sort of shuffle like Igor in Castle Frankenstein, careful of things on the floor.

When he bent and dropped the supplies at the foot of his bed, Avery turned on the lamp so he could see. His bookshelves, his dresser, the table, pictures on the wall, were all lit by the 40 watt glow. It was just bright enough to read a book in bed at night. What it didn't show was the little photo of Caroline taped in the shadows. It was the only picture he had of her, from back in elementary school when she wore a plastic flower necklace. He knew it was a little strange, but what could he do? It was all he had. What would they even talk about if that picture came to life? Horses, cartoons, or what she saw in a dream? Anyway, he could still see her in that younger girl. He would just have to get to know her now. In truth though, he didn't have the slightest idea how to talk to her.

He thought about that and how close he had been to her today, close enough to smell her flowery hair, and he realized he better have something to say. He needed a script. If today's meeting happened the same way again, he had to imagine things he could say. He could relive it and take the time to write what he should have said.

Avery sat down on the bed by his pillow in the soft light and opened the drawer below the lamp. He took out a pencil and a notebook and turned to a fresh page. He wrote at the top, *What to Say*. He drew a line underneath.

Moving the pillow behind his back, he stretched his legs out down the bed so his feet ended up in the rocket things. He tapped the blank page with his pencil. The photo of her looked back at him. She caught his eye... Horses, cartoons, dreams?

He wrote, *Hello.*

That was a given.

But depending on how she replied, it could lead to other things.

How are you?

That was opening the door even more.

Are you going this way?

Would she let him walk with her?

Are you taking a bus home?

Maybe she wasn't. Maybe someone was picking her up.

Aren't you glad it's Friday?

Did she have any plans?

Do you like rockets?

He wrote all that down before he realized he never introduced himself. He knew who she was, but did she know him? They hadn't been in the same class since 3rd grade and he doubted if she remembered him. Then again, that might be good; it was the sort of romantic thing someone on TV would say.

I remember you from 3rd grade.

That was good, he thought. She might even smile or laugh. They had been in orbit together for a long time and here they were at high school, finally meeting again.

FLYING SAUCER

Avery heard the old car stop on the driveway outside. His mother was home. He got off the bed and stuffed the note into his back pocket. That was a good start, he thought. At least Caroline wouldn't catch him tongue tied next time.

He clopped down the stairs as his mother opened the door.

"Avery?" she called.

"Hi mom."

"Did you eat?" She closed the door behind her. She was carrying a bag.

"Yes. We had fish and green beans."

He could smell the food in the bag she brought home.

"That's good," she said. "I'm tired." She took off her shoes and gave him a kiss as she passed him on the way to the living room. "What have you been doing?"

"Reading."

He followed her into the other room, to the couch where she sat down heavily. "Turn on the TV for me, would you, dear?"

He did. And they sat in the room with only the silvery glow from the TV and when Jonathan Winters came on they laughed at every turn of his mind, so funny and far from the ordinary he could have stepped out of a flying saucer on his way home from the Moon.

SATURDAY, October 13, 1962

APPLES

The Tweed apple orchard used to cover a fair amount of land. There were a hundred or so apple trees and even into the next century, when all those truck farms in the valley were tamed and paved and turned into housing developments and cul-de-sacs, there were still a few wild little pockets of land left where an apple tree still grew. The last of the line and stooped with age and nearly hidden in blackberry vine.

But in 1962, the Tweeds had sold the middle plot of land and what farm remained had to be tended by two people in their late sixties, their daughter-in-law and her son. It was no longer a working farm. They were lucky to hold on to what they had. They sold cider by the road and twice a week Eileen brought bottles to the IGA to sell on commission. Each cold glass had a label Avery had drawn: a tree holding an apple as big as the sun.

There may only be a few of those trees that grow in the 21st Century and if you're lucky enough to find one, the apples that grow on them are rare...Maybe fewer than ten appear a season. But if you see one, you'll see a smallish, hard, almost knot-like fruit, shrunken from what they must have been. Carefully twist that apple a couple times off the mossy limb, wipe it on your shirt and take a bite. That taste is unlike anything you find in a store. It turns so quick from tart to sweet, it's like electric current running in its juice. It's so peculiar and wonderfully alive if you gathered all the apples you could and squeezed them into a potent syrup you could run an engine off that fuel. You could probably shoot a rocket from that forgotten Tweed Farm straight to the Moon.

THE STAND

After a long morning crushing apples, Avery sat at the booth on Donovan with sore arms on the table, holding a book. He wasn't really reading. He was tired and distracted. General was on the other side of the street. He moved almost imperceptibly, like a big aquarium fish, watching Avery watching him.

There was a fair amount of traffic on that Saturday and cars would stop on the gravel shoulder to buy fresh cider from him. Avery kept the money in a cigar box and the glass bottles on the counter disappeared one by one. He also had the empty bottles at his feet that the regulars would bring back.

Avery stayed out there until the afternoon when his grandmother came to see him and relieve him. She brought him a piccalilli sandwich with cucumber and spinach greens. He gave her his chair while he ate, standing up, noticing that General was gone.

"Do you know that horse is older than me?" she told him, "Really and truly. When I was a girl, I remember seeing him, back when the woods still grew close around here. Then, if you weren't careful, you could go out walking in it and get lost. The trees grew so tall and tight they shut out all the light." The woods still grew thick upon Chuckanut Hill and even on a clear morning like today there would be tendrils of fog weaving slowly through the tree tops.

His grandmother fished out a dollar from the cigar box and tucked it into Avery's shirt pocket. "You go get yourself a treat," she said.

"Thanks, Grandma."

Another car pulled over and Avery gave her shoulder a touch as he left. He walked beside a muddy rut in the driveway. He could hear her behind him talking about what a nice day it turned out to be, October and still sunny warm. He smiled and squinted at the sun as her voice faded away. His grandmother called this an Indian Summer, the last burning light and heat of summer.

The driveway became the spot where their Pontiac spent the night and left a bruise of oil on the earth. His mother drove to the bowling alley at noon, so the house was empty again as Avery went in and up the stairs.

STARLIGHT

The window made his room an underwater blue. He turned the radio on. It was his grandparents' station, featuring music by the Dorsey Brothers, Ella Fitzgerald, the Andrews Sisters and Nat King Cole. There were also ads for dentures, life insurance and lawyers who promised the best benefits at the lowest price. Avery had not quite found rock 'n roll. Except for what he heard other kids sing in the halls, or played on diner jukeboxes, and the Beatles were still a year away. Besides, this station gave him something to talk about with his grandparents. His grandmother told him about songs she liked and the time she went to see Morgan Russman's big band, when the dance floor was filled with couples and the lights of the ceiling mirror balls twinkled on everyone like starlight. She told him about the rumba that played in Cuba where they married and outside their honeymoon room were palm trees and waves.

Avery sat at the table below the window. Everything he needed for rockets was waiting for him. First he cut squares out of tin foil then he rolled each one around a pencil to make a silver tube, ten of them. He taped the seams and crumpled a nosecone seal for the tops of each rocket. The other end he squeezed around a thin, inserted paintbrush to form a nozzle. Duke Ellington's orchestra played as he lined up the rocket bodies like sardines on the tabletop. They did look like fish. He even had a little box to carry them in. He carefully taped on paper triangular fins. He was good at making them. The next part would take longer. The rockets needed fuel.

He opened a box of matches and spilled them into a pile. This would take time, listening to Doris Day and cutting the match heads off with kitchen shears. They bounced and beaded together. They formed a red ant hill.

Another couple songs came and went.
He remembered the last time he fired a match head rocket.

LUCKY

Actually, it was three of them taped together. That was Howie Van Sloat's idea. He thought that would make it like one of those multi-stage Saturn rockets. It would be able to climb past the telephone poles and tree tops. And against his better judgment, Avery went along. He slid the experimental rocket onto the stick of its coat hanger launcher, positioned it just so, above the candle and he lit the wick. There was a bit of a breeze. Avery had to cup his hands around the flame. That's when it exploded. He wasn't even able to move out of the way. If he wasn't wearing his glasses, Avery would have got the fire right in his eyes.

He was lucky.

These were the first rockets he made since then. When he was done cutting matches, Avery carefully filled each rocket with the grains of phosphorus. He tapered the nozzles so the packed match heads couldn't fall back out the hole at the end. He hummed along with Benny Goodman as he put the rockets in their cardboard box. It wasn't exactly what you would expect from Cape Canaveral, but it would carry them safely to the highway tonight.

The music faded away like a leaf blown down the street and an old man started reading the news. "Prime Minister Fidel Castro has announced that Cuba is willing to trade the Bay of Pigs prisoners for the sum of 62 million dollars worth of medicine and medical equipment. Baseball's World Series has been postponed for the second time due to rainy weather in California. A telephoned death threat against President Kennedy today led to a police alert—"

Avery did what his grandfather so often did when the news came on—he stood up, leaned over and turned the volume down. Who needed more bad news? The music of 1942 still hummed in his head.

EVAPORATING

Out the window it was another blue sky October day evaporating. A huge V of geese went overhead, sounding like a cloud of school kids on recess. Avery left his rockets and went downstairs.

He thought he saw the ghost of their dog. It was a blur as golden as a smudge of sunshine on the floor by the door and it was gone the next second. Avery didn't doubt it could be real and he went to the door and opened it.

A dry leaf clawed over the sill. Off in the distance in the crisp air came the rumble and clatter of the highway construction. He thought of walking up Donovan to catch sight of them working. He could climb to the top of Donovan Rock and sit there and watch the yellow bulldozers, truckloads of crushed stone, graders and rollers, the steam coming from hot asphalt. It wouldn't take long before they plowed their way through town. Anything in the way would be flattened and turned into cement...Houses, gardens, parks, grocery stores, shortcuts and alleys, climbing trees and favorite fields. All so you could get somewhere faster.

Avery took a step outside onto the porch and he shut the door behind him. A flock of crows, cawing, were flying overhead. He covered his eyes as he watched them fleck across the bright orange sun.

His grandmother was gone from the cider stand on the road. Apparently some time had crept away from him while he was busy making rockets upstairs.

He jumped over the steps and landed with a scratch of gravel on the driveway.

A blue jay went squawking away from him through the alder. Now that he had committed and made the leap to the ground, he didn't know what to do. He could go to his grandparents for dinner or he could stay at home, heat up a can of soup and then go shoot rockets.

It was funny not knowing what to do. Standing there stuck like a tree in the ground. Being still made him aware of things like the breeze in the drying leaves, and the hopping birds making the branches tremble. He liked it. He felt he could turn into a tree and he wouldn't mind at all.

MILKMAN

Not far from him, a twig snapped under the hoof of General. The old horse had been watching Avery. Now its head was turned back in the direction of the road. The colors of day were fading into shadows on the gray and ghostly horse.

Avery turned on his heels and climbed the porch steps and did what a tree couldn't do. He walked inside the house, into the kitchen, opened a can and poured it into a pan. He stirred it, warming it over the blue gas flame until the soup was ready to eat. He took the warm bowl into the other room and turned on the TV.

Ernie Kovacs sat down in a cluttered low cellar with fireplace behind him. "It would be hard to find a better place to see a Lon Chaney picture tonight than here because, although it's true that I built this addition to the house, the house itself is the former home of Lon Chaney, and across the street, the former home of Boris Karloff. About the only thing missing—the initials of Bela Lugosi cut into the wine cellar."

The night was coming on fast and later, when Avery stood at the sink washing his dishes, past his reflection, the window looked out on a world turned dark. He set his bowl and spoon in the wooden drying rack. The house was quiet.

He might have seen that dog ghost again as he climbed to his room. Ghosts weren't anything new for him. Once he saw a ghost in his grandparents' house. He knew it was an Indian coming out of the woods from the past, probably walking an old trail that went right through the house.

Getting his box of rockets, Avery came back down to a house full of emptiness and shadows.

Avery left the light on in the hallway—he didn't

know how long he would be gone—his mother would probably be home before him. The hallway shined golden. She would be glad for a long wooden lane that wasn't booming with the roll and crash of bowling balls. She might even be asleep on the couch when he got back, the TV turned down to a whisper.

    Paused at the door, he put on a warm blue jacket. It was a present from Uncle Bill who used to be a milkman. Wearing that half a uniform made Avery feel like he was a milkman too—going out into the early dawn, leaving behind a sleeping family while he went out to deliver the day.

METEOR

It was chilly outside. The sunset had already disappeared, leaving the sky a deep colored sea. There were probably owls blinking out of their holes in trees.

It wasn't far up Donovan where the road split like a creek around the huge gloomy shape of the glacial rock too big to be moved, that had sat there since the last ice age, unmoved by the trees growing, getting cut down to make way for the town.

As Avery walked along the road shoulder, cradling the rocket box, he held out his other arm, palm open towards the rock and he swore he could feel it pulling him. Maybe it had some sort of magnetic property? Maybe it was like that meteor in *The War of the Worlds* and one night it would start to turn slowly open? He could have closed his eyes and known he was getting close to the rock—the air temperature dropped and the sound turned down.

Avery walked around it and expected to see a coyote up on top, watching him with red coals for eyes. There was plenty of room to lie down up there. He had done it often by himself, on his back, staring at the depth of the sky. Cars and trucks would go by and nobody knew that you were up there. He hurried along the gravel.

The road got steeper and then, where it flattened into a field, Avery looked south and saw the highway. There were round red lights lined up where the work had stopped. The machinery was sleeping. There were a few farmhouses with lights on low but Avery walked in the dark.

He could see three dim silhouettes standing like they were on a dock. Tony and Harold and someone else, moving about the red glow and soon Avery could hear them too, laughing and talking.

"Hey, Tweed!" one of them called. "Is that you?"

Avery nodded. Then, because it was dark, he added, "Yes." He carried the box before him in both of his hands like an astronaut taking careful steps.

CANDLELIGHT

They were up on the edge of the highway, a couple feet off the ground where a tangle of rebar poked from cement. The blinking red lights were set on saw horses and Tony hopped on the back of one. "You got the rockets?"

"Sure."

"Well, come on up. Watch your step though. Here," Tony reached for and took the box from Avery so he could use both hands to safely climb.

"Is there ten?" Harold asked.

Avery hopped around the bent, twisted metal framework and stood next to them. "Yes."

Tony already had the box open and they were peering at the rockets.

The other boy, older than them, took a look too. "They're puny!" he laughed.

"This is Jerry," Tony told Avery. "He's a senior. He drove us here in his car."

Jerry plucked out one of the rockets and held it between his fingers. "I bet these don't even work."

"They better work!" Harold said. "We paid him two bucks."

Jerry laughed again. "Oh, man."

Harold laughed too and Tony punched him in the arm and said, "They'll work."

Avery took a wooden skewer from his pocket and looked for a place to be the launch pad.

"Right here," said Tony. "This is the spot. We can shoot them off the end."

Avery bent and fixed the stick in a cement crack. He ran the rocket down it and put a candle just beneath it. They had him a little worried though. He didn't want it to fizzle. His hands shook as he lit a match.

Jerry the senior smirked and put his hands to his ears. "Tell me when it's over," he joked.

The candlewick flamed and began to heat the rocket nozzle. Avery took a step back, just in case. The other boys did too, just in case, even Jerry who was three years older than them.

NOWHERE

The candle went out. A tiny breeze, no bigger than a breath, had put it out.

"Hah!" Jerry swept his hands from his ears and pretended to hold a camera, taking a picture. "Priceless."

"Hang on," Avery said. This time he struck a match, he kept his hands guarded around the candle. Maybe the rocket would blow up. He hoped not.

He tapped the rocket hooped to the skewer so the candle flame burned directly into the rocket. The match heads had to catch any second.

Tony said, "Careful."

Suddenly there was a throaty whoosh. It sounded like a miniature furnace, a real Atlas rocket made very small. But that was it. The rocket went nowhere.

Jerry and Harold were laughing like it was some great comedy act on television, as Avery crouched and slipped the rocket off the stick. The tinfoil was hot to the touch.

"Here," said Tony. "Try the next one."

Avery went through the same procedure again, only this time he wished the rocket would be a shooting star over the dark landscape doomed to become a long alley of cement to Canada.

The second rocket coughed and hopped a half foot, enough to clear the skewer and fall.

The third rocket made a nice orange flame, melted a pool in the votive candle and died on the stick.

The fourth rocket only barely out-jumped a frog.

Jerry moved into the red danger lights glow and waved his arms. "This is too rich. This is painful."

Harold agreed, "Yeah! I want my money back!" He pushed Avery's shoulder. "Give my money back, Tweed." Like a tough gangster, he shoved a hand into Avery's shirt pocket.

"Wait!" Avery reached for him. "That's not your money! That's from my grandma. She gave me that."

Harold wrestled the dollar away and Jerry stepped in between them.

"Settle down! Listen, what difference does it make? I've got some real rockets in my car. Come on, let's go for a drive."

DINOSAURS

Jerry started towards the darkness on the fresh surface of highway behind them. His car was parked next to a trailer filled with gravel.

"It's my Grandma's money," Harold whined. He passed the dollar to Tony and trotted off to catch up with Jerry.

Tony put the dollar in Avery's box with the remaining rockets. "I'm sure some of them would've worked."

Avery accepted his box. "I know."

"You want to see what Jerry's got?"

Avery shrugged.

"Come on."

So Avery tucked the box under his arm. He could hear the rockets skitter about loose in there like a handful of moths.

They walked around the big wheeled trucks and tracked vehicles. Some of them looked like tanks. The moon made them all weird as sleeping dinosaurs.

Ahead of them, Jerry's car started with a roar and its headlights went on, blinding Tony and Avery.

"He's got his own car?" Avery asked, shielding his eyes.

"It's his parents'. It goes pretty fast though."

Jerry revved the motor as the two boys hurried around to the back doors and got inside.

"Hey, Avery," Jerry said. "Why don't you pass me one of those rockets for a cigarette?"

On the front seat beside him, Harold snorted.

As soon as they were seated, Jerry spun the steering wheel and gave it gas. The tires screeched, the car pointed south at the miles of new road that ran smooth to Seattle. Jerry weaved the car through all the machinery and stacks until there was nothing but finished road before them.

Harold let out a whoop and pounded the dashboard. "Let's go, let's go, let's go!" he howled.

SPEED

The road ahead of them gleamed smooth as ice and the speedometer swept clockwise faster and faster. They were going sixty, then eighty, then as the car hit 100 mph, the machine floated on a cushion of air. Harold laughed hysterically. Avery clutched the upholstery. It felt like he was on a magic carpet the way the car seemed to breathe off the road. He knew that even though the highway was clean and clear for miles, all it would take was one pile of gravel or a curb dropped in front of them and the car would explode and tear out of reality. With his eyes closed, he prayed. He could feel his heart beating.

Jerry took his foot off the accelerator. Left to the drag of wind, he let the car slow by itself. The long red needle of the speedometer pointed at the numbers going down. The air poured around them and the blur of dark land became something friendly again…The silhouettes of hills and trees, the dot of a farmhouse light.

Harold clapped his hands and laughed. He was babbling something to Jerry but all Avery could hear was the merciful chop of their coasting wheels.

Avery looked out the window beside him and wondered how far they'd gone, past Acme or Custer? He didn't know. "I want to go home," he heard himself say.

"Hah!" said Harold.

"I want to go home," Avery repeated.

"Alright. Relax, Rocket Man," Jerry said. "We'll get you there." The car was down to 20 now and he gave it some gas. He was looking for a road they could pull onto. He pointed to the dashboard and told Harold, "Why don't you look in the glove box."

Harold popped open the dash compartment. He dug his hand in greedily. "Bottle rockets!" and took out three.

Tony leaned over the seat to see and hold one too.

"Wow!"

"Now what do you think of old hotrod Jerry?"

"You're the best!" Harold told him.

"Amazing!" Tony agreed. "Can we shoot one?"

"Be my guest." Jerry found a spot to turn off the glassy highway. It was a muddy lane chewed by Caterpillar tracks.

Half a chimney stood in the debris where a house had been. The highway came in so fast it hit it like a tornado. The remains reminded Avery of a story he heard. Somewhere along here was a house where the people refused to leave. So the highway paved right over it. The family still lived in it like a submarine.

Tony held the bucking wheel, "Once we get back on the road, roll the window down. Point and shoot."

Harold grabbed the roller handle though his hand slipped and they all bounced around as the car jostled along the cut tracks. They were in a clearing where trucks must have been parked, but the headlights found a road behind a heap of brush and dead trees.

Avery saw a deer watching them, off to the edges of light, like a garden statue.

The car picked itself up onto concrete and Jerry turned the wheel hard right.

WAR

Harold quickly unrolled the window. The air that poured in was sweet and cold. "Hey, Rocket Man! Pass me the matches!' he held an opened hand back over the seat, fingers snapping.

Avery opened the lid of his cardboard box. His rockets were tumbled together with loose spilled match heads and a dollar bill, another candle, skewers and he found the matches. He put them in the impatient hand.

Tony showed Avery the bottle rocket he held. Even in the gloom of the backseat, Avery could tell that factory-made rocket was going to burn into the sky.

"What do I do?" Harold asked. "How does it work?"

Jerry said, "Just light the fuse. Hold it by the end of the stick, out the window and aim it away from the car."

"Shoot it out the car?"

"Yeah, like Buck Rogers."

Harold laughed. He lit three matches before, with a hiss, he got the fuse lit.

"Out the window! Out the window!" Jerry pointed, hand off the wheel.

"Okay, okay!" Harold squeezed the end of the stick the rocket was attached to and stuck his arm outside.

In the next moment they saw the rocket, trailing a shower of red sparks, streak over the hood of the car, down the narrow road in front of them.

"Hell's bells!" Harold gasped.

Tony tugged his arm, "Give me the matches! I want to try!"

"No! I'm the expert."

"Give me a try, Harold!"

Jerry said, "Relax, ladies. There's two left. You can each fire one. However, allow me to suggest something."

They quieted down to listen. The old road they were

on shook the car. It was nothing like the new highway. It rattled with the memory of old automobiles and farm vehicles.

"It's a little game I like to call War. Wait til you see another car coming the other way, see?" Jerry pointed at the dark road ahead of them. They were heading back towards town, it wouldn't be long. "When you see the headlights, get the rockets ready. Your timing has to be just right."

"Let me switch places," Tony told Avery, "I have to sit on that side." He crawled over Avery and opened the window to the road. The car was filled with a bat-like breeze of October night wind.

Avery took a look out the window at the highway on his right. It was a moonlit clearing and he could see the construction flattened low like a snake on the ground. Wherever it had moved left rubble and the remains of trees ripped up and crumpled in piles. He saw the lighted window of a house it had crawled over. Was that the house someone still lived in underneath? He turned to look out the back window.

"Do you have any more matches?" Tony asked.

Avery had one more paper matchbook and when he passed it he got another look at that sad jumble of rocketry.

The road took a bend. There was a tall screen of fir trees and a car passed them in the other lane.

Tony and Harold scrambled with their matches. Tony got one lit but he dropped it.

"That one snuck up on us," Jerry said. "We'll get another chance." He braked them through some more corners. Another car appeared but Jerry held up his hand. "Relax."

The woods flashed with deep shadows. The car swung through another tight couple of turns. They were down

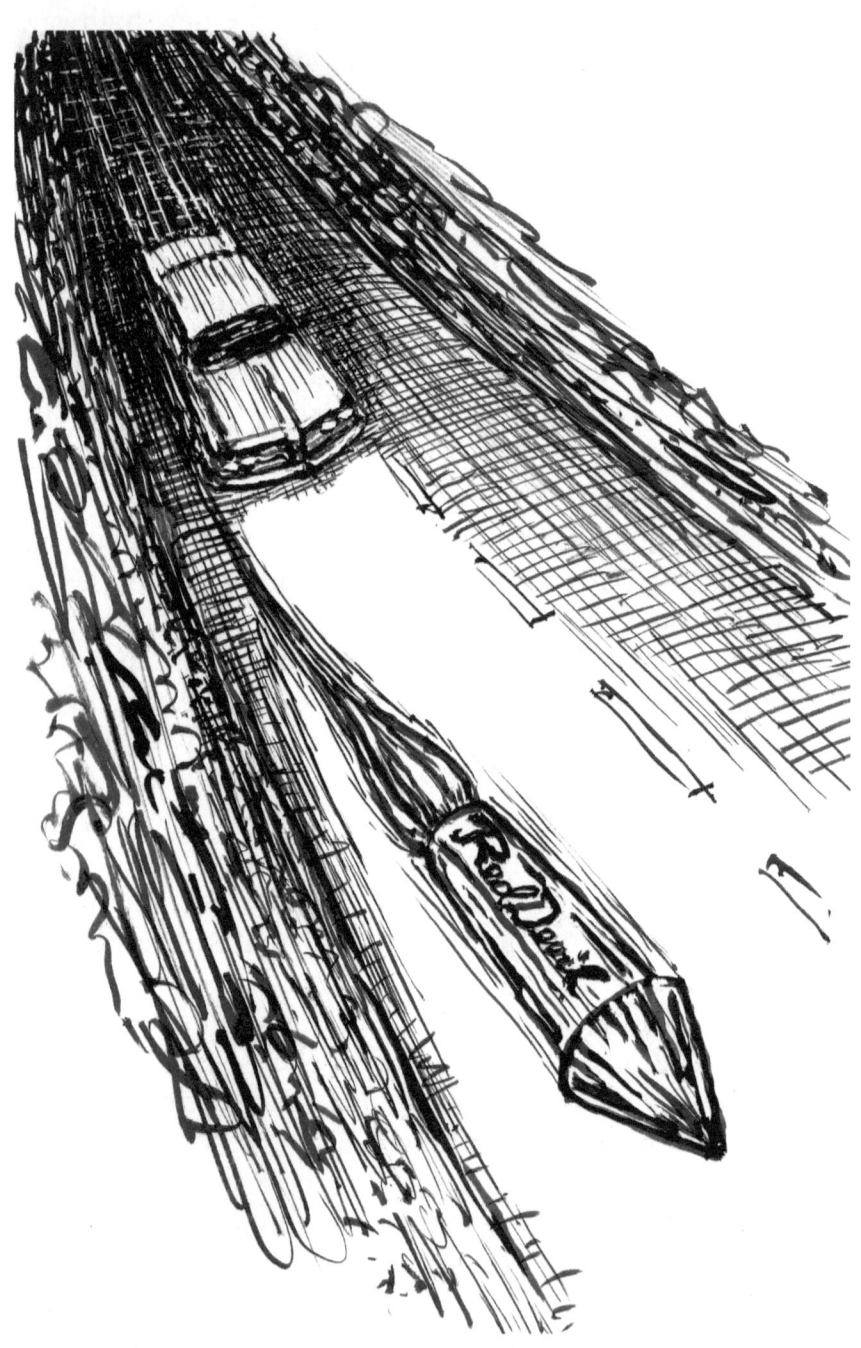

at sea level now. Water and islands showed past the trees.

After one last turn they were on a straightaway and Jerry pointed down the road. Two beads of light showed way ahead of them. "Okay. Here comes your target."

Avery kept silent as they prepared, as Tony held the match ready to strike, with the rocket on his knees, the wind blowing in. It smelled like high tide, like they were on a pirate ship preparing a fusillade.

"Light your rockets!" Jerry ordered and they did. The fuses hissed. Harold plunged his arm out the window, pointing across the hood while Tony leaned into the slipstream.

Harold's rocket made a wild red trail over the windshield, as a shower of bright sparks lit the back seat.

"I got it!" Tony yelled.

Harold threw his stick out the window and turned in his seat to see what happened on the road. "He's stopping!"

Tony screamed, "He's turning around!"

Avery looked back too and he could see headlights spin across the open clearcut as the car spun into their lane.

"He's following us!"

Jerry punched the gas pedal. "Well, he's not catching us!"

Avery could feel his heart beating away again. He put a hand on the vinyl seat in front of him and clung to it.

"He's gaining!"

A couple houses blew by. They were getting close to town, they had to slow down. Tony could see the chrome grill of the car behind them gritting its teeth.

"Hold on!" Jerry yelled. He hit the brake and the car skidded onto a split in the road.

Avery shut his eyes as he thumped against the door. This was turning into one of those shows he and his grandfather would watch—two cars chasing high speed through a city.

"He's still there!" Tony called.

"We'll lose him," Jerry said. "Hold on!"

The car screeched and shuddered again. It swerved and pitched as Harold screamed, "Hold on!" The wheels dug into the dirt shoulder and they popped back onto the road, engine yowling. Somehow Jerry kept the car from spinning out. They just missed a mailbox on the other side of the road as they skidded and wagged like a salmon fighting upstream.

Avery held his breath. He could feel the cold presence of death and his eyes were shut. He was barely there.

The car rocked around another corner and this time they hit something that cracked and scratched along Tony's side of the car. They went over a big bump and everyone bounced, hitting their heads on the ceiling. The car slammed to the ground with a bang, suspension snapping like bones.

As if it was nothing, Jerry shut off the headlights.

BAYVIEW

It was a miracle they were all still alive.

They were in the right place if they had died. Around them was the Bayview Cemetery.

The car crept along past a row of headstones. Tony rubbed the back of his neck and looked out the cracked back window. "We lost him."

The radio had gone dead. Jerry cussed. His parents' car wheezed. He could barely turn the steering wheel. "I think we better stop here," he said and they did.

Tony tumbled out his door. Avery's wouldn't open. It struck against a marker in the grass. He had to crawl out the window, holding his rocket box.

Jerry slammed his door and swore. The car responded with a billow of rising smoke from under the crumpled hood.

Harold had difficulty getting out. He held his elbow, his face soured. "I think I broke my arm."

Jerry ignored him. "Look at my car!" It looked like a giant bear had clawed the left side. Smoke continued to billow out of the rumpled seams, spreading out across the mowed cemetery lawn. Jerry was up to his knees in it. But his troubles weren't over.

Headlights rayed overhead and the boys turned to see a car stopping where their tracks led bursting and scraping the ground.

"He found us!" Tony yelled. He ran, followed by Harold, still gripping his arm.

The car door up there on the road slammed and Avery ran. Not after Tony and Harold, Avery ran at the cemetery as if further in there a deep crypt might be willing to pull him in and hide him. He cut between graves, knowing he was running over tombs with flowers that seemed to hiss at him and it was all in black and white like one of Count Misfit's horror movies.

There were yells from back at the car and suddenly an explosion. Avery saw his shadow running in front of him. He didn't stop. He ran over it as it got dark again, crunching in the dry leaves beneath an oak. Scared as he was, he had the strangest feeling that he wasn't really there, that he was just breath inside a boy's body as it ran. There were probably plenty of ghosts like that floating in the cemetery air.

Avery did know the way home though. He had been here before. His brother and father were buried further down the hill towards the ocean. All he had to do was follow the slope of the hill, up and out and back onto Donovan. He hoped Tony and even Harold with his hurt arm were finding safe passage through the cemetery. It felt safer for him anyway. He slowed to a walk and gave a nervous look over his shoulder.

ANGEL EYES

He didn't see any glow from a burning car. He was beyond seeing it now. The cemetery had taken him on a route of dips and turns past trees and mausoleums. Everything behind him was night. Ahead of him the crowds of stones climbed down towards the valley and the air between the trees shimmered with the movie light of the Drive-In, just beyond the cemetery wall.

He slippered through some more fallen leaves and in a dark hollow he froze.

Ahead of him, standing on a tall marble block was an angel.

She had frozen too. She held flowers clutched to her chest, her head was bowed, looking at the sad ground, and her big wings were held out behind her in silence. The wind blew back her long hair and the folds of her dress. But it was her eyes that froze Avery. They glowed.

An angel in a cemetery, greeting him with glowing eyes? For a moment Avery wondered if she had come for him. Was he already dead? Maybe he died in Jerry's car and, like one of those *Twilight Zone* episodes, he didn't know it yet. Rod Serling would step out from behind a tombstone with a lit cigarette and explain that Avery had found his next stop. Of course it didn't happen that way

There was a simple explanation and Avery remembered. The angel's statue eyes were daubed with glow-in-the-dark paint. It was no mystical omen, someone would keep her eyes fresh with a new coat; it was a town tradition. Avery had heard about it. He had just never seen it before. And what a night to have her appear—eyes brought to life by the Drive-In next door, and the moon above.

Avery walked around the statue. She did look like she could spread those big wings any second and carry

him away. He wondered if he would even mind if she did. There had to be another world where the bad things that happened here didn't occur. As long as Caroline was there too.

MOONLITE

As Avery left the cemetery, climbing over the low stone fence, he looked back and remembered the play *Our Town*. The shadowy blue scene was just right to recall the school stage where he watched that cast of ghosts return to life and stare out at the audience.

He crossed a field. He could see the big slanted screen of the Moonlite Drive-In seeming to jump with images that shined. There was a tall hedge and wavery wooden fence that circled it, but from here you could sneak up on it like another world, silent, already in progress.

There were a few cows regarding Avery as he crossed their field. Their black and white hides rippled with the movie glow. They must have watched a lot of movies standing there, late nights spent digesting monsters, car chases and comedies. A rustle in a pile of blackberry—was it a mouse or a rabbit who must be watching too? Some nights in the summer, Avery would bring a chair to this field outside the Drive-In walls. With a transistor radio you could tune in the sound and hang it on the armrest and it was just like an invisible car parked there. Since the summer, he and the cows had seen *Mysterious Island, X-15, Thunder Road, The Greatest Show on Earth, GI Blues, The Curse of the Werewolf, The Road to Hong Kong, Journey to the Lost City, Bad Day at Black Rock, The Errand Boy, Journey to the Seventh Planet, Premature Burial, Night Creatures, Tales of Terror, Lonely Are the Brave* and *Moon Pilot*.

It was almost like landing on another planet. A gigantic slice of black sky was filled with Jimmy Stewart watching over Avery and the sparse landscape he shared with creatures that fed off the glow.

Avery saw Jimmy Stewart row in the fog in a little boat with a boy. They must be lost, he thought. They looked awfully small and hazy on that big cloudy screen.

Avery could also see the roofs of the cars parked in rows like cemetery stones. It was such a peaceful scene he took a deep breath of it, reminded how lucky he was to be alive. The 100 mph rocket race and crash could have been the end of it all.

Off in the direction of downtown, he heard a siren. From the dark woods a coyote replied.

SUNDAY, October 14, 1962

MASKS

On Sunday morning Avery caught a ride with his grandmother downtown. She parked the boat-like Oldsmobile on Harris Ave in front of the pharmacy. The road was slanted and ran like a waterfall straight down to the shipyard, the cannery and the sea. She and Avery parted ways on the sidewalk. He wanted to wander around and she had a prescription for Warren to pick up. She gave him a wet kiss on the cheek and squeezed his arm.

Whatever happened to all that blue sky? After a few months of summer, people got used to it. This October day had hid it away like a sea snail gone deep in its gray shell.

Avery's white sneakers flapped on the steep pavement. He passed the window of Coast to Coast Television and Radio Repair. It was closed, the TVs turned off. He kicked a pebble and it skittered off onto the street, caught by a tuft of clover.

In places on all the streets, the asphalt was cracked or wearing thin and weeds were growing through. 9th Street had a green layer of moss from disuse. Trees were starting to grow in the empty lots. Buildings were left unfinished, second stories with beams exposed and unmade walls. This part of town had been only half-built, only half awake in a dream between its past and what would happen next. It seemed like it could go either way—back to forest, or become bricks, concrete and businesses. It was hovering. And Avery liked this in-between state. He liked to explore the vacant lots and the buildings time forgot.

He passed the closed Terminal Store, its old white paint cracked on the bricks. You could look inside and see the soda fountain, the long beveled mirror on the back wall with the bullet hole. He stopped on the corner and crossed 11th Street. Cobblestones emerged from the fading coat of asphalt. He could feel it right through his shoes—that other era when there were horses on this street pulling carts down the hill to the docks crowded with wooden sailing ships.

A pair of seagulls landed on the roof of Odd Fellows Hall. Those birds wandered up and down town in the air or building to building like skeletons, always searching. He wondered if they remembered, if they passed their knowledge on. They were such strange creatures, part of a cursed landscape, expressionless and always hungry and ready to unfold wings to fly away if you came too close to talk to them. The gulls on top of the hall watched him and one of them screeched. The lonely cries of it faded as Avery walked below the angle of their sight.

The big window of the hardware store was filled with Halloween masks pinned to a black hanging curtain. They lined the glass display in rows, there must have been fifty or so. There were monsters from Count Misfit movies, presidents, animals, ghosts and heroes. They were made of flimsy plastic, almost see- through, with holes where eyes would be. If it wasn't nearly Halloween, you would wonder what that strange vision meant.

SUNSHINE

Avery passed on by. Trick or treating was years from him now. They used to get in the car and go up South Hill to the big houses there. His quiet back roads and farmhouses had only shadows to hand out. They had plenty of apples though. It would be a good way to clean the trees, to send every little trick-or-treater up on a ladder. Help yourself.

The sidewalk ambled along an old vacant brick building. Wooden shudders were nailed over the windows. It seemed to be holding its breath, hoping not to be noticed, so Avery looked at the cracks in the sidewalk and waited for the corner.

He could hear two things coming up the steep street. One was a heavy, steady beating like a heart and the other was a trumpet. Even though the two sources might be blocks apart on Mill Avenue, they played together like a song from a living creature humming off a roof.

The first sound was easy enough to find. It breathed out an open door, below an awning that read Sunshine Printing.

Avery stopped in the doorway. A man stood at a big iron printing press, working it himself, in tune with the machine. The platens moved like metal wings as he turned sheets of white paper. The man in there seemed to dance, standing on one leg, pumping a pedal with one foot, pulling a lever with one hand, as he manually fed paper beneath a pounding flat plate of gleaming steel. It was like a steam engine, wheels and cogs and levers were turning and he was like some Jules Verne hero guiding it on. With one hand he kept the wheel of the printing press turning as he stacked more pages on the table beside him. Avery watched from the doorway, quiet as a birdwatcher as the silvery platen folded up wings, landing, and the man pulled the last sheet of paper off.

The walls of the room were covered with posters. They must have been made here for fifty years. Avery was staring at a green one, weathered by age. *Saturn Circus* letters curved above the drawing of an elephant in a ring. Below it were more faded letters, jostled like in a wind, *Bringing Joy and Cheer to a Troubled World.*

"Hello there."

"Oh," said Avery, "I was just walking by."

"You heard the old Cleveland Chandler & Price." The man patted his machine and smiled. "Come on in."

"What are you making?"

POETRY

The man held up the sheet of fresh printed paper. "You like poetry?"

Avery shrugged. It was one of those things they made you memorize in school.

The man couldn't help laughing at that look. "I know," he said. "This isn't like what you get in school though." He spread the sheet on the stack with the rest. "These are the pages for a new book of poetry."

Avery came over closer so he could see the poems stamped cleanly into the weave.

"Do you know the poet Perry Roberts?" Even as he spoke, the man was moving again, there were things to do, the book couldn't sit still. "He lives here in town. This is his first book." He was restacking the pages flush in the corner of a huge paper cutter. The blade of it was like a Medieval sword. "Actually," the man stopped. "He's not far from here. Would you like to bring him a book?" He reached to another table and picked up a fresh blue clothbound book.

Avery didn't know why he took the book from the man. Poetry had never really stuck with him, but something happened when he held that blue book and read the title embossed in pale yellow letters on it. *Floating Almost All Alone.* What a name for a book. What could be inside? Avery felt he was holding some sort of mystery and also felt that it wanted him to know, wanted him to open it and read.

"You know where the Lo Tide is?" the man asked.

"On the water?" Avery pictured the beach off Poe's Point when the ocean swept out and it was thick mud you would sink in, white bits of shells and piles of weeds and driftwood.

The man laughed. "No, I mean Perry Roberts is at

the Lo Tide. Go down the street on 10th, next to Horizon Books on the corner."

"Oh, yeah. I know that place." He knew Horizon Books, he had been in there lots of times before. The Lo Tide was sort of a shadow tacked against it. It was more likely to be noticed out the corner of your eye. "How will I recognize Mr. Roberts?"

"That's easy. Just look for a big owl. You can't miss him."

"Okay."

"He'll be very happy to have the book."

"I'll find him."

The man put his hand on the cutter blade. He was anxious to get back to work. "I appreciate the delivery. You'll get a kick out of meeting him. He might even make a poet out of you." Lining up the cut, he brought the blade down with a crash as Avery turned and left Sunshine Printing.

FOSSILS

Avery liked the feel of the book cover in his hands. His fingers couldn't help running over it. The sound of that trumpet hovering over the bricks was gone. Maybe it had flown on like those geese and swans you saw these days trailing south. There were other sounds, gulls again, and along the bay the sound of train cars rumbled.

Avery followed a coppery green stain that ran downhill. It came from the old rainspouts that had been pouring rain on the sidewalk for over fifty years. The stain sparkled. It looked made of shattered crystal ball. Would there be fossils in that old rain? He wondered if you could get close with a microscope and see frozen moments, the memories of old black tin cars, handcarts filled with luxuries brought by sail and even further back, the thick forests so dense you couldn't even walk through, when it was only a wet mountain mist sighing in the leaves. Where the ancient water mark trickled off the curb, Avery crossed the street.

Horizon Books stood on the corner. He thought he might even go in there afterwards. He still had a dollar from his grandmother and that bit of rocket money—enough to buy a couple sci-fi books or fantasy paperbacks. They also had a box of free books and sometimes he found something good.

Beside the golden painted brickwork of Horizon gloomed the doorway to Lo Tide. Avery had never gone in there. It had the look of one of the taverns that sprouted like mushrooms along Harrison on the way to the docks. He heard that long train cry as it left town.

Avery stopped in the entryway before the door. Along the sidewalk two circular windows watched from the wall like eyes, but with the curtains pulled he couldn't see inside. The doorway had a bad smell to it. If it wasn't for the book in his hand, Avery wouldn't have gone in. It seemed hard to believe he was about to bring such a beautiful book of poetry in there.

LOBSTER

The door handle, a metal cleat for tying ships to land, was ice cold. Avery imagined there must have been places like this in seaport towns all around the world, wherever sailors wandered ashore. His grandfather must have been to a few.

The Lo Tide on a late Sunday morning wasn't a busy place. The one big room was kept dark, lit only by red and green lamps on the walls and candles on the empty tables. With the curved cedar slatted ceiling, it felt like being beneath a turned over boat. But the man in the print shop was right—it was easy to spot Perry Roberts—short cropped hair and thick glasses, he sat alone at a table in the back, hunched, with his hands wrapped around a white mug.

As Avery approached him, Perry's eyes never flickered from a spot deep in that cup. Avery stopped when he got close to the round table and he said, "Excuse me. Are you Perry Roberts?"

That was when those eyes slowly eased out of the depth and regarded Avery. They blinked once. "Did something happen?"

"No. Nothing happened. I brought your new book." Avery tried to pass it to him.

Perry stirred. He moved like a very old man though Avery knew he probably wasn't the age of his grandfather. He was just old before his time. One hand left its clutch on the mug and reached for the book. His hand trembled like the candle flame. "Look at that," he said. He took the book and his other hand raised to hold it too. "Did JB give you this?"

"The man at Sunshine Printing did. He said to bring it to you."

"He did a good job, didn't he?" Perry got the book

open and turned some pages. "It's a real beauty." He paused at one of the poems he knew. "And you brought it all the way here?"

"Yes sir."

The owl eyes were on him again. "I don't suppose you've ever been here before. What do you think of this place?"

Avery gave another look around the room. "It looks like somewhere a moth would go during the day."

Perry chuckled He turned a few more pages and got to the end, where a black woodblock sun was stamped. "What books do you read?"

"Oh...I, I like science fiction mostly."

Perry nodded. "Different worlds, different Americas..." Holding the book in one hand, he reached into his gray suit jacket and took out a pen. "What's your name, son?"

"Avery."

Perry set the book on the table and opened it again. Holding the first page, he set the pen on the paper and it wrote, seeming to move by itself. "I want you to have this, Avery."

Avery stared at that book held out to him and he stammered, "I don't know much about poetry."

Perry nodded and shrugged. "Sometimes it takes a while. Sometimes not." He was glad when the boy took the book from him. "You know that bookstore next door?"

"Horizon."

Perry nodded. He got something else from his coat pocket. He uncrumpled a ball of dollar bills. "You go in there and get the *Anthology of Western Literature*. It's the biggest book you'll see, sort of a field guide. Start reading poetry, Avery. Watch for the Frenchman who walked a lobster on a leash because it knew the secrets of the sea."

Avery held the book in his hand again. He was about to speak when the door opened and a white rectangle of light showed. Avery recognized the silhouette that entered and walked their way.

"Avery? What are you doing here?" It was Dallas Clay, with a cigarette going in the corner of his mouth.

"Hello, Mr. Clay." Before Warren got sick, the two of them used to go deer hunting out in the county. Dallas had that hard worn look that was used to death. Avery knew he had been in the war, at Guadalcanal, and whatever happened there never really left him, especially not his eyes.

Perry Roberts picked up the slack, "Avery brought me a copy of my new book."

"Is that right?" He looked back at the boy. "How's your grandfather doing today?" The smoke came out the side of his mouth.

"He's okay. I had breakfast with him this morning."

"Well, you better run along, Avery. I have to talk with the Professor here."

Avery saw those owl eyes slowly close out of what Avery guessed was shame, as he bent his head, clasped his cup and took a drink.

"Say hey to your Grandpa from me," Dallas said.

"Yes sir." Avery backed away. He waved the book, "Thank you, Mr. Roberts." It looked like the poet was going to say something back, but Dallas moved in between. His red plaid hunting jacket blocked them as he leaned over the table to speak seriously.

DAYLONG

So Avery left the Lo Tide. He didn't realize until he stood in the white daylight again how fresh the air was outside. It was another atmosphere. As Avery shadowed along the yellowy bricks of Horizon, he wondered, *what was Dallas Clay doing with Perry Roberts?* He could ask his grandfather, maybe he knew. And did his grandfather know Mr. Roberts too? Had they been hiding poetry from him all this time? Avery smiled. Now it was too late. He held the blue book of poetry tight to his coat.

There was a window full of books beside him. He ran his eyes across the new covers. *Travels With Charley, For Love, A Wrinkle In Time, Silent Spring, In the Clearing, Something Wicked This Way Comes, The Man In the High Castle* and then he was before the green painted door.

A long string of bells clattered as he entered. It was hard to believe this big room full of books and Handel's *Water Music* was connected by a wall to where Perry Roberts sat roosting in the dark, but it was. In one hand, Avery had his first poetry book and the other held the money waiting to turn into the history of poems from Greece to Harris Avenue.

And it was that Sunday, whether Avery knew it or not, he became a poet. That Sunday took him on the mile long walk home on Donovan between the valley farms, past the PT-109 and other landmarks until at the end of his daylong journey he lay under the vault of his roof, waiting for sleep.

Beside him, his alarm clock ticked time towards Monday morning. He had his two books of poems on the nightstand, Perry Roberts on top of the thick anthology.

He remembered the look his grandfather gave him, and how his grandmother and mother both acted so shocked and repeated, "The Lo Tide!" when he told them where he'd been.

"Avery, you can't go in there!" his mother said.

"I was only delivering a book." Avery showed it to them. He tried to explain its effect on him. "And anyway, how does Mr. Clay know Perry Roberts? Do you know Mr. Roberts too?" he asked his grandfather.

His grandmother got up nervously to take the emptied potato bowl to the sink, where she ran a little water into it.

Warren held his fork as if he wished it was a cigarette above the food he barely touched. He chose his words carefully. He walked around them. "Dallas takes care of Perry Roberts at night when Perry needs someone to look after him. When he's not a teacher at the university, Perry Roberts goes a little crazy. Dallas keeps an eye on him." Warren stared back at his food, peppered the way he always used to like it. With a dab of hot English mustard on the greens, it was only missing the vapors of a cigarette.

"Honey, you shouldn't be there with that man," Avery's mother told him.

"I just brought him his new book from the printer and he gave it to me. As a present."

"Is anyone ready for ice cream?" Eileen opened the white freezer door.

Avery turned on his side in the dark. Above him, on the cold dry shingles, he could hear the start of rain.

MONDAY, October 15, 1962

FUGITIVES

Someone lit a fuse, the hiss of early morning rain on the leaves, the sparking raindrops on the creek. Avery was waiting for the yellow bus to pop from Donovan Rock. It was a sort of optical illusion the way it happened every school day.

Avery stood awkwardly, coat slick wet cradling the thick anthology under his layers to keep it dry.

The heavy machinery sounds carried in the wet air. of Bulldozers and trucks, the engines and wheels; a clanking and scraping and crunching and pounding like that giant from *Jack and Beanstalk* in the sky. They seemed closer than ever.

Avery wondered how much they built in a day. After school, would the bus drop him off on the edge of a highway?

When he saw the bus emerge from the rock, he took a step back off the road into the rivets of gravel, the little stream the rain made. Even that miniature world by his feet was subject to constant change—bugs he couldn't see were running out of the way as their land cracked with water and the footprints of a giant's tennis shoes.

The bus gave a shrill wheeze as it halted and opened its door. Climbing the steps, Avery felt the thick book move under his coat like an animal he kept safe from the weather.

"Hello, Avery."

"Hi."

Past the driver, halfway down the aisle, he heard his name called again. "Avery!"

The climate in the bus had steamed his glasses up, but Avery turned his head and saw Tony waving hands frantically at him. He was holding back some important news; he was practically falling in the aisle. Harold slipped across to the seat on the other side.

Avery remembered the rockets on Saturday night. He supposed that's what it would be about, but after Sunday it just didn't seem to matter to him anymore. He was still cradling his book of poetry as he took a seat next to Tony.

"Did you get away?"

Avery stared at him. Wasn't it obvious? Wasn't he here with all the rest of them, soaking wet and packed in seats like sardines? He took off his glasses and rubbed the lenses clear.

"Did you hear what happened to Jerry?"

"No."

"Did you see the newspaper?"

"No."

Tony shook his head in disbelief. His voice got lower even though the bus was filled with laughing and conversations were just as steady as the motor sound. "After we took off, Jerry's car caught on fire."

"I thought so."

"That car we saw on the road up above us was the police. They took Jerry to the station. I don't know if he told them we were in the car too. We might be fugitives!" In his excitement, Tony dropped his metal lunchbox.

"Oh great..." Avery shut his eyes.

"Anyway, at least me and you are okay. Look at Harold."

Avery opened his eyes and looked across the aisle where Harold sat glumly, staring at the green seat in front of him, with a cast on his arm. There were already a few signatures on the white plaster though rain had smeared the ink.

"We just have to lay low for a while," Tony said. "And hope Jerry didn't squeal."

Avery shut his eyes again. All of a sudden, getting on this bus had taken him away from poetry and driven him right into a gangster movie—only without Bogart, George Raft or Robert Ryan—this one starred three high school freshmen, one with a broken arm, one with a lunchbox and one concealing poetry.

Avery watched the Gull gas station out the window. There was actually a seagull perched on top of the blue sign. He almost said, "Look!" but they were already past it, going over the bridge, and anyway he didn't know if Tony would think it was that funny. Harold surely wouldn't. He looked like he would give anything to have never seen a rocket. He looked like his arm belonged to an alternate reality where bad things happened to people who were just trying to have fun.

"So if anyone asks," Tony continued, "We don't know anything about Jerry and we were all at home on Saturday night, right?"

"Sure," Avery said. He could see their school approaching, getting bigger in the bus windshield down the aisle. He was sure Tony would be looking over his shoulder all day and checking the parking lot for squad cars, but Avery was already thinking of something else, someone he remembered like poetry.

MEANING

Avery spent the whole day at school that way. If he wasn't looking for Caroline, he was thinking of her. In Astronomy class, he let outer space drift away. Funny—ten years later, he would be traveling back to this very moment to write a poem. If he had the eyes for it, he could have seen himself hovering overhead.

With his hand to his forehead, he could keep an eye on her through the narrow window between his glasses and fingers. The world condensed to just that view. There was a poem in Perry Roberts' book and a sonnet by Shakespeare. He had to write something down. He had to take the note out of his pocket and add something to his list of what to say to her when he got the chance. He wrote on it carefully, cupped behind his hand, *Do you like poetry?* Then he pushed the paper back into his pocket.

When the class ended that was all the writing he had done. He closed his textbook, stacked the anthology on top and filed out.

Tony caught his arm in the hallway as Avery floated in the hallway.

"I didn't see you at lunch."

"I was in the library," Avery said.

"I saw Jerry. He didn't tell the cops about us. He told them he just lost control of the car. We're in the clear!"

"Okay."

Tony laughed. "Okay? Man, you're a cool cucumber! You've got guts, Avery."

They moved back into the crowd for their last class. But it wasn't really that Avery felt that courageous on Saturday or about the fallout since—he just found something on Sunday that gave him more meaning.

TESTING

The only scare of the day was waiting to happen in the next classroom after he took his seat at the worn yellow desk, about fifteen minutes in.

The intercom crackled on. Normally this only occurred in the morning before classes started and they would stare at that contraption on the wall as it droned like a beehive.

The morning bulletin included a reminder about the Friday dance. For it to buzz into life at this time of day meant something out of the ordinary was happening.

It was the principal's voice, not a student reading memos. He said, "In preparation for the possibility of a nuclear attack, we will be conducting a drill. We must all be ready so we know how to save ourselves if the attack comes. Knowing what to expect will save your life."

In that moment between the next words, Avery wondered where Caroline was. He closed his eyes.

"There will be a bright flash, brighter than the sun, brighter than anything you've ever seen before. Then there will be a huge explosion, a wind of broken glass, walls and roof will tumble, and the force of it could throw you and hurt you. There will be burns if you are exposed. The blast can burn you worse than a sunburn. You will only have a moment, your only hope to survive an explosion like this is to duck and cover. Roll yourself under the desk, tight as a ball—there is no time to wait. Always remember, a flash of an atomic bomb can come at any time, wherever you are. Stay covered until the danger is over. You will be told when it's safe. Today's signal that the test is over will be the ringing of the school bell. We will begin with the same bell, starting...Right now."

The bell rang and everyone jumped.

"Under your desks!" Mr. Humphreys called. "Duck

and cover!"

All the chairs chirped and scratched as they went back. Avery folded himself into that wooden cramped space. He stared at the gray linoleum on the floor, the flecks of gold and black, until the bell stopped. Then he closed his eyes. You would have thought there would be talking or some nervous laughter, but the room was quiet. Everyone listened.

They heard the rain brush the window. They heard the glass tremble with a gust of wind. They held their breath, waiting for the flash of light that would fill the room. Then their town, with the farms and trees and houses and stores would all be wiped away. Avery thought of the streets he knew, the Drive-In at night, his grandparents' house by the pond, the orchard, his room and Caroline with her hand he never got to hold. Her eyes he never got to look into. How awful and stupid to lose the whole planet because people couldn't learn to love what was right in front of them.

This wouldn't be the end though—Avery told himself, taking a breath into his sleeve—at least he was in the same building as Caroline. He could find her in the rubble. She would be scared but okay. She would be overjoyed to see him and hold him like a girl in a movie. They could start over without the school or the people that let this happen.

The rain and wind tested the window a moment longer. Then the bell rang.

The principal congratulated the school and said, "Having this drill is proof that we take the threat seriously and I'm sure that had an attack really occurred, we would have been just fine. Teachers, you may now return your classes to their studies." The intercom gave a click and resumed silence, becoming once again a sort of quiet robot face, watching them from the wall.

Mr. Humphreys wheezed as he emerged from his desk at the front of the class. He steadied himself and straightened his rumpled suit. "It's okay, class," he said. "You can take your seats," and he watched them pop up one by one around the room. A few of them were laughing now. His eyes, after darting around at the signs of them all settling again, stopped on the book on Avery's desk. He couldn't help noticing the way the boy kept a hand near it and once when he turned from writing a long passage on the blackboard, he saw Avery reading from it. Mr. Humphreys held his hand up to quiet the classroom.

"We are very fortunate that wasn't real," he began. "Although the weather report does call for high winds by this evening, I think we'll survive." He took his glasses off and cleaned them with a handkerchief. He did that several times a class as if his eyesight needed to be constantly refreshed. "I wonder though, before we continue where we left off before the war, I think this might be a good time for a poem. I don't mean to call attention to you, Mr. Tweed, but would you do us the favor of reading us something?" He noticed the stricken look on Avery's face and hurried to explain, "I hope I'm not putting you on the spot. That's not my intention. We've just been through a terrible war, humanity has been shattered, and you have the healing gift of poetry."

Avery couldn't stop his hand from shaking as he placed it on the book and drew it to him. Already there were scraps of paper in it bookmarking pages and there were thousands of words in there to read but he took a deep breath and turned the book open. He didn't like everyone watching him but he knew it wouldn't be him; he knew it would be the poem talking. Nervously, his voice pitched like a green tall reed, he began.

CONSTELLATION

By the evening, the wind that had been driving around the town all day, first as a bicycle then as a car, finally turned into the engine of a steam train. It moaned and roared and shook the house. It held the house and tried to twist it out of the ground. How could something invisible that lived in the air go so crazy? It was mad as a canning jar full of bees, shaken up and set to whir like a gyroscope.

Avery lay in the dark and listened and held his breath every time the wind climbed up another notch, as if just a little bit more was all it needed to tear the chimney off and cleave the roof like a clamshell ripped free and shucked to the side. And every time it rose with the sound of an angry wave, it would crash to the ground, snapping branches loud enough to be a whole tree or a rolled over car. The iron sound of the storm kettled and steamed.

He wondered what he would find in the light of morning, thrown down on the ground. The news loved those stories of strange birds carried miles off course. Last year, a pelican was found in Liberty Park. Maybe this time it would be a silver airplane, a TWA Constellation with snapped wings and bent propellers hanging in the trees lining Chestnut Street. The startled passengers would climb down ladders to the sidewalk. Maybe they were expecting Hawaii or California. They would be standing there with their suitcases, wearing short sleeve shirts and flowered skirts, just as odd as that pelican.

Somehow he fell asleep and somehow the world didn't come apart while he was sleeping.

TUESDAY, October 16, 1962

WHAT TO SAY

Although it did look like a bad dream had gone on the rampage...Everyone on the bus ride to school was pointing out disasters. There was a tree down on the road. They had to creep around it. The tires cracked the limbs, the branches scraped the windows. The PT-109 was split

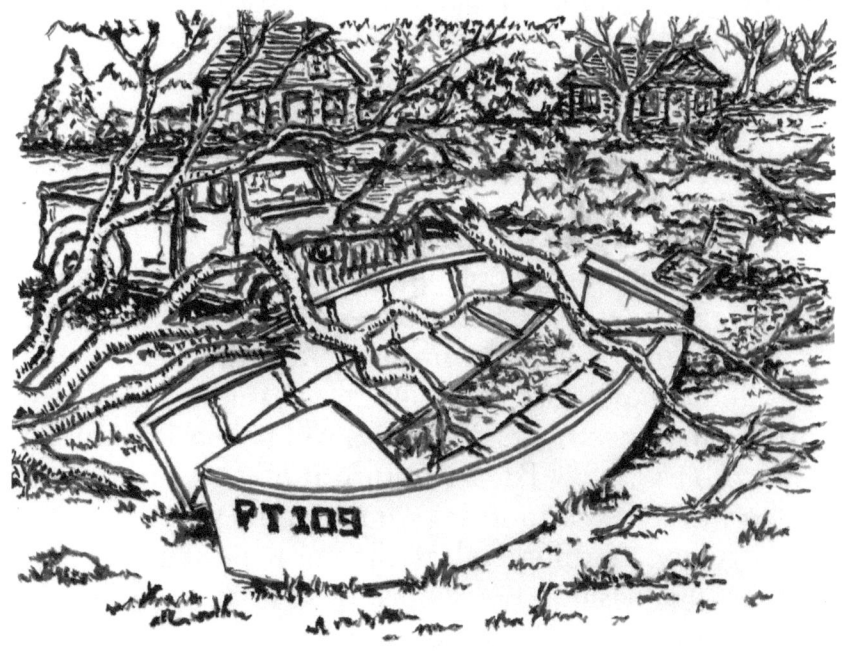

in half. A utility truck was parked by a snapped telephone pole, restringing the wire from a huge spool. The man on the ladder looked like a puppeteer. The fence surrounding the Moonlite Drive-In had blown down. You could see all the speakers planted in rows and the tangled swing set in front of the screen. The trees in the cemetery stood in shock up the hill. A science fiction doomsday movie could have filmed from the bus, narrated by Vincent Price all the way to the journey's end.

The school looked gloomier than ever. The oak tree

on the lawn in front had lost a big branch. Two of the windows were broken and taped over with cardboard. It looked like a castle that had been under siege. Still, as they got off the bus, Avery could hear a robin singing. He held tight to his book and followed the cement, the stairs, the linoleum and wood, the shiny hallway that led to his classroom. With some time before the bell, he opened his book and read. He jumped around in it from Grendel to Robert Creeley.

It wasn't much longer after the teacher said good morning when the intercom speaker crackled and interrupted. Everyone stared at that mask with the voice coming out.

"Welcome back," the principal said. "I'm sure you noticed that our school did not quite blow away last night. But there have been some damages. We appreciate your patience as we clean up and restore the building and grounds. I apologize especially to the students in Room 109. Those two broken windows will be repaired during lunch break. Now I'd like to turn it over to Janet Olson who will read this morning's announcement."

"Good morning. At least the storm didn't damage the school gymnasium. Remember, this Friday is the Homecoming Dance and in case you haven't made your plans yet, or have trouble working up the nerve, here are some anonymous suggestions supplied by one of our very own students. This is entitled, *What To Say*. 'Hello. How are you? Are you going this way? Aren't you glad it's Friday? Do you have any plans?'" She paused as if she could sense the laughter building throughout all the rooms. And it was too; in Avery's class there was a ripple of giggling. Her voice continued, even in the halls it carried, echoing. "'Do you like rockets? I remember you from 3rd grade.'" She stopped again. Avery tried his best to hide his embarrassment, but he could feel his face heating up, red as a beet. He even tried to laugh along with the rest of the class. Harrison was in stitches, he slapped his desktop like the sidekick in a movie. "And last but not least, 'Do you like poetry?' Well, you can bet our anonymous Romeo does," her voice laughed. "I hope this list of conversation starters has been helpful to the rest of you too. And we'll see you Friday at the dance."

The intercom died and the class was still muttering and laughing. A boy told a girl across the aisle, "I remember you from 3rd grade." She laughed and said, "Do you like poetry?"

Avery stayed quiet. He had already checked his pockets and discovered his note was gone. It must have fallen out yesterday. Nobody would know it was his though, he told himself. The intercom called him an anonymous Romeo. So why worry? He told himself, it was just more wind, wasn't it?

It was sort of funny in a way—what he was too nervous to say to Caroline, she heard along with everyone else in the school. He could have had his notes painted on banners and dragged across the sky by airplane.

The teacher was bringing the class back to history, writing on the blackboard, but Avery was still thinking about what happened. Maybe it was good it happened. He didn't know what he wrote was so funny. What if he said any of that and Caroline started to laugh? Mary Barnes laughed when she said, "Do you like poetry?" But he was sure Caroline wasn't like that. He just knew she was different.

FLOATING

After class he went through the day the way he always did, only now he carried his poetry book everywhere he went and when he saw Caroline it was good and when he didn't see her, he waited. He supposed he needed to start a new *What To Say* list. He would have to give it some thought. Maybe he wouldn't need one? Maybe the words would just come to him like someone in a movie.

That's when he had his chance. It was just like it had been planned, like some unseen mastermind as all-powerful as the wind had pushed them to this spot.

Caroline walked towards him. Avery actually heard a song he loved from the old days radio and as the distance between them closed, step by step, he didn't have time to consult his popular *What To Say* or even remember romantic movie lines. All of a sudden she was there.

"Hi," Avery said.

Her eyes darted from the crowd to him. "Hi."

She was going by, the music was playing and starting to fade, he had to act fast. "Do you like poetry?"

She slowed, surprised and brushed a brown strand of hair off her cheek. She smiled briefly and he knew it had been the right thing to say all along.

Someone moved in between them and like one of those streams he used to watch flow and break through a dam of stones and debris along the gulley in the field, another person and another followed. They were standing in a blur. And the bell rang and their moment in a dream was over. That was how it felt to Avery anyway. As he passed through the rest of school day, he was floating on air. He was one of those white October clouds that was quite content to find itself pushed along by the wind. Being a cloud was nice and easy and at 3 o'clock it took him right out the door.

SPLASH

The storm had left the air fresh and clean as a piece of cut pine. Avery thought of walking home, but was pulled along into the yellow bus that would drive him home instead. That was fine. He read his book.

Even if there were words he didn't understand, he was like a bumblebee with the gold pollen sticking to him, turning pages, soaking in the forms, finding the poems that made him stop and repeat like a mantra in his head.

At the top of the hill, when the bus opened its door, Avery got off, even though it was before his stop in the valley below. The wind had torn down branches and snapped tree tops. He walked along the side of the road as the bus pulled away. The ditch was filled with leaves and brown water and other debris tangled the flow. So many of the leaves had been ripped free he could see down into the valley that summertime hid in green. He could see the roof of his grandparents' house. And he caught a glimpse of the gray pond out behind. He was glad that pool hadn't blown out of the ground. It could have been scooped in a big coffee can and poured in a culvert a mile away. He would have to go looking for it, listening for that old frog to find the pond again.

There was still some breeze, but now the storm was just a memory—the wind talking to itself, telling everyone what it used to be.

Avery turned left onto Hickory. Of course the anchor was still there and the blue station wagon. He went down the path, crunching seashells and kicking branches aside. The yard didn't look too bad though. There was still enough light to get an hour's work done.

The house seemed awfully still. The yellow kitchen light was on, but it looked like a painting of a house. When he rang the brass ship's bell, it made a cold metal splash that sounded way too loud.

His grandmother hurried to the door, straightening a dark blue sweater. She looked worried and barely opened the door. "Oh, Avery. Your grandfather's had a bad day. He's not feeling well at all. He's trying to sleep."

Avery heard a horrible dry cough. He took a step backwards. "Well, I was going to see if I could help pick up some stuff around your yard."

"Aren't you nice?" She gave him a smile of such relief Avery took a step towards her again.

"I'll just get a rake and work until it's dark."

"Thank you, Avery." She looked back towards the kitchen at another racking cough. "I'll make you some hot tea." She put out a hand and squeezed his fingers.

"Okay."

The door shut. The string from the bell swung like a noose and Avery moved away.

The rake was in the shed behind the house.

It leaned against the table saw. There were still signs of his grandfather's last project, the halved hull shape of a model sailboat he was going to mount on a stained square of cherry wood backing. Avery ran his hand over the smoothness. It wouldn't take much to finish. He thought of coming back sometime to do that, as he took the rake and carried it outside.

The birds at the feeder scattered, but they would be back. Halfway up a tree, a squirrel watched him, head down, tail flicking.

By the time Avery raked two big piles together, his grandmother came outside carrying a plate. "Yoohoo!" she called.

Avery dropped the rake in the brush.

"I made you some tea. I brought some cookies too." She held out the plate. "Wasn't that storm a doozie?"

"How's Grandpa?"

"Oh," she sighed. Her eyes started to tear up. "He's pretty sick, you know. We went to the doctor yesterday and it wasn't good news."

Even outside in the breeze with the birds, a chainsaw from another farm, and the distant sound of the highway construction, you could hear a cough now and then caged in the house.

"And he doesn't like what is happening. Soon he won't be able to do the simplest of things." She touched her eyes with a handkerchief Avery didn't even notice she was holding. "Drink your tea, dear. Have a cookie."

Avery took a hot sip of Lipton that she mixed with milk. He held the plate balanced on his arm like a waiter.

"It's starting to get dark. Would you like to come in for some supper?"

"No," he said. "There's something I've been thinking about. I should go home soon." He dipped a gingersnap in the tea and took a bite.

She watched him eat. "Try not to worry about your grandfather. I know it won't be easy. There's not much we can do. Try not to be sad though."

"I know."

He finished his tea which was good and warmed him while they stood there in the cool yard. Shadows had crawled down from the trees and covered the ground. They said goodnight. Eileen took the plate and cup and Avery picked up his coat and the book placed on top. He returned the rake and followed the pale shells back to the road.

When he looked back, the kitchen glowed brighter. There were other lights on in the valley too. They weren't alone.

NUMBERS

Avery walked Donovan back home. Better to take the road than fall into some uprooted bramble or fallen tree he couldn't see. The full moon of Saturday sat on a torn cloud, the bright white sand on it turning to shadow.

The air smelled of apples. Hundreds of them, knocked to the fields, and each breath was like a glass of cider.

Avery looked for General on each side of the road. He hoped the old horse made it through the storm. Sometimes when he was out on nights like this, Avery would see the gray blue of General stuck like a raindrop on the window. Surely that wise old animal would know where to go to get out of the wind. It made Avery think of all those birds singing around town in the day—when night came, they just seemed to disappear from sight to somewhere safer.

Ahead of him, the little porch light blinked in the passing branches. Avery stepped from the asphalt onto the gravel and mud of his driveway. There were some white slivers mixed in, a few buckets worth of Poe's Point clam shells and mussels. A few summers ago, Avery thought he could make the whole driveway look like a carpet of Moon, so it would shine and crackle like his grandparents' path. It didn't take him long to realize how many years his grandmother must have gone to the seashore and back and there were so many other summer things he'd rather do.

He called hello to the dog who wasn't there and went inside. He went straight to the lamp in the hallway and turned on the light. Before he could try to stop himself with nerves or second guessing, he set his poetry book on the cupboard and took the phonebook out of the drawer below the telephone.

It was strange how thinking of Caroline would turn

him suddenly into a bubbling teapot. He tried to get ahold of himself. He was only looking at letters in a book. They happened to be alphabetized into a word that became a last name, that's all. Big deal, right? The book was filled with them. Still, there was no way around it, reading her word made him tremble. Maybe he was too full of poetry.

After he breathed deep a few times, he read the phonebook again.

There was a slight problem, he noticed. There were four families listed with her same last name. Which was hers? He didn't know her address, so those details of streets didn't matter. He would have to call each one and ask if she lived there.

"Does Caroline live there?" he tried out loud.

He cleared his throat and tried something else, "Is there someone named Caroline at your house?"

He closed his eyes. When he opened them again, he picked up the receiver and dialed.

It rang and rang and nobody answered it. With some relief, Avery hung up.

He found the next number. He had to redial as he did it wrong.

When some old man answered, "Hello?" Avery instantly began.

"Yes, I would like to know if there is a Caroline who lives at your home?"

"Is there a what?"

"Caroline."

"Care of what?"

"Caroline!"

"No. No, there isn't." The old man broke the connection.

Avery could see the hard-of-hearing old man returning to the muffled world he lived in, where all the sounds crumpled like walking in the snow.

There were only two numbers left. "Is Caroline there?" he said. That sounded better, more relaxed, short like a haiku line. "Is Caroline there?"

He picked up the receiver, held it against his ear with his shoulder while he read the next phone number and dialed.

A girl answered, "Hello?" It could have been her, he didn't know. He didn't find out. He quickly hung up while the sound of her voice was still a breath in the air.

ARMOR

He didn't sleep much that night. His nerve had failed him. An hour of raking branches and leaves on Hickory Hill, going over and over in his mind what to say and the second he heard her voice he melted. With all that time to lie there and toss and turn, he wished it would have been different. He thought of the *Route 66* he watched before bed.

"Do you know anything about frogs?" Buz asked the girl when they sat on a bench together in a black world, a sort of cemetery of bare land with white trees in the background. And then later on when they were tired outside the city limits and had a campfire going, he told Tod, "She's carrying a whole town on her back. Who know for how long? Betcha she never loved anybody. Course she hasn't. She's fallen out of the armor like the hermit crab and got lost. The armor that keeps marching, and sword that keeps swinging. That's the trouble with fighting a war, you see; you get so wrapped up in fighting that you forget how to make peace." The girl, lying on the dark ground with the frogs and firelight, turned away from them, pretending to be sleeping.

When he did fall asleep, when the dream machinery finally took over, he was staring at Donovan Rock. It was stamped with a giant bear paw, painted red and black and white and Avery knew it was an Indian image. He had seen that same image on the Salish cedar boxes and baskets and masks in the museum downtown.

He wasn't sure what it meant. In his dream he just watched it happen. And when he woke up, he looked at the ceiling. He looked at the window with the curtains drawn. The green dial of his clock told him it was almost the next day. He closed his eyes and thought of Caroline until he fell asleep again.

WEDNESDAY, October 17, 1962

BETTER

When his mother woke him, coming upstairs at 6:30, he sat up and told her he couldn't go to school.

"What's the matter?"

"I don't feel good."

She sat on the edge of his bed and felt his forehead.

"I feel sick." He put his hands over his stomach.

"Oh dear." She brushed his hair with her fingers and kissed him. "I better call the school." She stood up. He wasn't sick very often. She paused on the stairs. "You don't have an exam today or something?"

He shook his head.

"Ok, honey." He listened to his mother creak down the stairs. He listened and could picture her turning on lights as she went to the kitchen and poured water in a pan then set it on the stove. It would take a while for that water to boil. She would return to the hallway any moment, look through the telephone book, find the number for the school, and call the office to report that her son Avery Tweed wouldn't be there today.

He wasn't sick though. He just couldn't go to school today. If only he could have said hello into the phone! Maybe he wasn't the poet he thought he was. The words failed him. It would be years before he could write poetry, could make every line the branch of a tree.

Anyway, he was already awake. He couldn't lay in bed and watch the day start the window and let his dark mood go on and on.

He put his glasses on, stood up, careful not to bump his head on the slope of the ceiling, and he took a blanket with him down the stairs.

The living room was dimly lit by the kitchen. Avery landed on the couch and stretched out beneath his blanket. He sighed. He was lovesick, that was it. But he couldn't tell anyone that he was feeling his heart. Nobody would understand. It was love that was so important to the life of the poets in his book. So shouldn't it be that way with him too? It's also a little bit crazy, he told himself, like Don Quixote and Dulcinea.

Maybe that's what he should do—ride General to school like a knight with a garbage can lid shield and a blanket cape and a saucepan helmet. They could stop on the damp grass below Caroline's window and Avery would throw out his arms and recite the poetry of his heart.

A laugh came from beneath the blanket on the couch. He was glad he remembered Don Quixote. He was glad his book wasn't all Petrarch's shining Laura, and Orpheus on his journey to hell. Avery felt better enough to crawl from his covers. He turned on the TV and returned to the cushions.

The picture formed in the wooden box. There was J.P. Patches in his shack planted in the middle of Seattle's City Dump. He was talking with Gertrude, a bulky mop-headed clown who also bore a resemblance to the show's other characters—Boris S. Wort and Ketchikan the Animal Man. J.P. rushed Gertrude out the flimsy door and told her, "Don't forget to call me later," as he tossed an oversized telephone receiver after her.

Avery laughed out loud.

"Avery?" his mother appeared in the kitchen doorway. She set her hands on her hips. "Are you feeling better?"

"No. I just couldn't help laughing. It's J.P. Patches." The clown was holding a rubber chicken to his ear.

"Well, I already called the school. I'm not going to tell them you've had a miraculous recovery."

He said, "I haven't." And he put his hands over his stomach. Imagination could make anything real.

She took a sip from her coffee cup and watched him. The room flickered with the cartoon light of an old Betty Boop cartoon.

After his mother returned to the kitchen, Avery realized she was right. He wasn't exactly playing the part. He got up and said goodbye to the city dump and turned the TV off.

Back on the couch, he tented the blanket over himself and closed his eyes. Now he was believable. He was The Haunted Shroud, the ghost of lovesick poets who spent his days and nights doomed to look back on the love he never had. And all because of that phone call...

Then he thought of showing up at school with J.P. Patches' giant telephone prop. He could tell Caroline, "I made a *big* mistake when I called you last night." Or better yet, what if J.P. could tell her how Avery felt? Like Cyrano, the clown would know just what to say.

Avery remembered Caroline's smile when he asked her if she liked poetry. Tomorrow, he yawned and promised himself. He would catch her where they left off. Thinking about that, he fell asleep.

PRETEND

When he woke, a silvery blue light filled the living room. He felt much better. If there had been any dreams, he couldn't recall them. Sometimes that was better. For example, that bear print painted on Donovan Rock—what had that meant? He stretched and stood up.

Out the window he could see their orchard and his mother picking up branches and leaves. So much for being sick, he thought and he went upstairs to get dressed and lend a hand.

He worked with her until noon when she had to get ready for the bowling alley job. The fresh air had revived him and his labor had provided the yard with several big brush piles. While his mother was inside the house, Avery walked out to the road to get a look at the rock.

His dream was still so real, he knew what to expect. It would have that painted claw. He imagined that's how it did look a couple hundred years ago. On the last snaps of white seashell and mussels, he stopped and looked up the road out of the valley towards the highway construction. Donovan went around the way it had for a while. Nothing looked out of the ordinary. The same gray and mossy surface breached the asphalt like a whale. A light brown car braked as it drove around.

Avery retreated off the road, out of sight with his rake held like a canoe paddle. It wouldn't be good to be spotted. Tony said they had truancy officers who would patrol the area looking for any kids out having fun. That car might have a net in the trunk. As it went by him, the netting would spread out and Avery would be trapped and pulled out of his driveway like a salmon. He played it safe and ran.

It was okay though. He knew his fear wasn't real. He just liked to pretend.

He slowed to a walk when he got to their car. There were some red leaves stuck to it like starfish. Maybe they were, he thought, maybe his mother was The Ancient Mariner stuck in the Coleridge poem? She was forever driving through the sea each day, to the bowling alley in the bay.

FORCES

After she left, he did some more work outside, keeping watch for General who was still unseen and he even had time to read some of his book. The highway clanked and pounded like an army getting closer and closer. When he got hungry he went back inside.

While he was eating his sandwich, watching the Dialing For Dollars movie, one of those moments occurred. They happened just often enough to make him aware that maybe something or someone was behind the scenes, pulling the strings.

The host for Channel 12's movie of the day appeared on the screen and said, "We'll return to *No Greater Glory* in just a moment, but first let's make a quick phone call and see if we can give some money away. Before we do, remember today's number and cash amount." A card flashed on the screen and then the scene returned to Art Pedersen. He stood at a table with a big fishbowl in front of him. There was also a telephone.

Avery had seen him dial that telephone before. He remembered Caroline's smile and bet she would like it if he called her sometime—once they were friends—and pretended to be Art Pedersen. That would make her laugh, he just knew it.

Art babbled on as he took a scrap of paper from the glass bowl. "These are all numbers from our very own local telephone book." He chose one and held it up. "If you're lucky, I may be about to give you a call. I hope the lucky recipient remembers today's number and cash dollar amount."

Avery said, "Number 5, $864!" This part was always exciting. Wouldn't it be great to win? What would he do with all that money? For starters, how about an actual rocket from the hobby store?

As Art Pedersen finished dialing the last number, the phone in the hallway suddenly rang.

Avery yelled and jumped off the couch and ran for it. On the second ring, he clunked the heavy receiver against his ear. "I know what it is!"

There was a pause. "It's your mother, Avery."

"Mom!" He couldn't believe it.

At that very moment, only seconds ago, two electrical impulses were charging through the telephone wires, head to head, nose to nose. It had taken place like a horse race, perfectly timed by someone or something.

Avery barely registered why his mother had called. It certainly didn't seem the equal of $864. He told her okay, he would go to the pharmacy and pick up the medicine for his grandfather and yes he was feeling better and he could hear the noise of the bowling lanes as she said goodbye.

The living room was waiting for him not with a parade, only with those ghostly 1934 children playing at war. He turned the TV off and they went away. They were alive in one less television. Whenever they drove by the TV station on Ellis Street, Avery looked up that tall antenna tower and thought of the people, the places, and all the stories streaming out of it into the air. There were invisible forces everywhere.

STORIES

He wore his green quilt jacket on the walk to town. It wasn't raining anymore but it was cold. Walking along Donovan, he stopped at the fence where a flock of goats gathered. They came closer to him as he held out dandelions. He loved their strange eyes.

And further on, at the top of the hill, he thought he caught sight of General down by the Carlson's chicken coop. But it could have been a low flying cloud.

On Highland Drive, he cut across to the cobblestones on Harris. The old trolley tracks took him to the pharmacy on the corner of Finnegan Way.

A Halloween display filled the window, rubber bats flying over a graveyard of candy bars and monsters. Inside, the smell of pine and soap and the floorboards creaked and sang like a sailing ship. Avery passed the wooden shelves filled with boxes and bottles. He gave the round metal bookstand a turn, spinning all the paperbacks as he went to the counter at the back wall. That's where Gordon the pharmacist stood in his apron, talking to a customer.

Sometimes Avery would come in to hear his stories too. He liked the way the old man could make a picture in your head, as real as a TV show. Gordon remembered everything clear as a bell—when the circus trains used to come through, scandals and strange characters and tragedies too. It did make Avery wonder what would happen when Gordon was gone. He noticed the way the old man's hand had begun to tremble—when he held a photograph it shook like the wind would soon blow it away. What would happen to all that history stored in his head? Avery would remember some of it and turn some of it into poems much later on, but most of those memories were part of another life that couldn't last. It would drift off in a stream. Gordon understood that though. Once he told the boy, "I know it sounds unbelievable, but when you're as old as me you'll be able to look back too and your stories will seem just as amazing to the next young person listening."

Avery approached the counter and waved.

"Hello, Avery," said Gordon. "Your mother telephoned and said you would be here." His hand rested on the big metal cigar lighter on the counter. It had been there since the start of the century and ever since Avery first noticed it, Gordon would let him click it and make the bright flame shoot out the top. Nowadays it was just for invisible cigars. Gordon let Avery light it for luck. He felt he needed it too, after all that was happening. He closed his eyes and made a wish.

Gordon held a white paper bag, but before he handed it to Avery, he said, "You better make a wish for your grandfather too."

Avery nodded and closed his eyes again. He heard the click and whoosh of flame. His wish was a prayer delivered by that rocket flare. Just let him get better, he prayed.

"That's a good one," Gordon said. That's what he always said, but this time, more than ever, Avery hoped he was right.

"Well," Avery said, "I better go." There was a lady waiting behind him.

"Come back soon," Gordon said, as he passed him the bag.

Avery nodded. He could feel the heavy shape of the bottle in the bag. There were also a couple of smaller bottles that rattled with pills, he guessed. He hoped it would be enough.

MOVIES

That bag was on his mind all the way back along Donovan. He switched it from hand to hand. He tucked it under his arm and he even imagined himself into that late night movie he saw a couple weeks ago, where Cary Grant had to fly medical supplies over the world's tallest mountains and the plane was sputtering and barely scraping over the icy pass. His grandfather's life was poured together in this paper bag. Once he made it to Highland again, the hill began to descend and he pretended the airplane he was in could start to glide.

The propeller feathered slowly around, the wind whistled by...He radioed ahead to the valley below, "Calling Hickory Control. Hickory Control, can you read me?" and as the wall speaker crackled with his voice, Caroline would push past the grizzled radio operator to grab the microphone, "Avery!" she would call out to him tearfully. "Avery, is that really you?"

He knew it was still a kid thing to do, but he liked pretending there was an airplane around him, wings sprouting from him, little green dials bumping and spinning as he turned the wheel slightly to keep him on track beside the deep ravine of the ditch beside the road. And he imagined Hickory Road was the runway. His plane engines stalled and coughed towards it and he could see the tiny shape of Caroline waving to him. It was one of those scenes in more than one movie.

When he did get to Hickory, when he did scuff his shoes along in that dust and gravel and taxied onto the seashell path, the movie stopped as he rang that brass bell. The chime was raw and cold and stayed pinned in the air until his grandmother appeared at the door. For a moment she looked right through him as if she'd been looking at ghosts all day and he was just one more. When he held up the paper bag and said hi, the life came back in her eyes.

"Oh, Avery. What a day this has been. Come in," she said.

He pulled open the maple colored screen door.

"Your grandfather has been asking for you," she said. She rubbed the quilted back of his jacket.

"This is from the pharmacy."

She took the bag and set it on the kitchen table. "Warren. Avery's here."

Avery heard a sound from the bedroom, a clearing throat that said, "Oh good."

"You can see him," his grandmother whispered.

SALMON

The kitchen was lit by a lamp on the table, but the bedroom was dark except for what light came in through the window past the alder tree and the blue gray of late afternoon.

His grandfather lay on the bed. He made it up on an elbow then sunk again when Avery passed the white door frame. He held out a hand and took hold of Avery's.

"Hi, Grandpa."

"Hello, Avery."

Avery could see that half the life had been let out of him. His voice sounded like a trickle of what it had been.

"I'm glad you got here today. It's not easy for me to get up and around anymore."

"How are you feeling?" Avery said and right away felt like a fool for asking.

His grandfather smiled though. "I've been better."

"I brought you medicine."

"That's good." He saw the boy was having a hard time. He saw how Avery had to look out the window and bite his lip. "Listen, Avery. I want you to know..." He looked at the glass of water beside the bed. It was a long way off. "Remember that time last year we went to Chuckanut Creek to see the salmon? They were coming back upstream after being out in the sea. Some of them were already dead on the bank. Some of them were so old they were covered in white. You remember how they still fought that water to get where they wanted to be?"

Avery nodded.

"I'm already there." He coughed. He cleared his throat and continued, "I don't want to have to keep fighting though. I want to be done now. I don't wish to keep losing ground and falling behind. That's why some of those salmon just throw themselves out of the water.

Right?" He shut his eyes for a moment. "It's okay, Avery."

Avery nodded again. His grandmother stood behind him and she put her hands on his shoulders.

She said, "The medicine makes him tired."

Warren's eyes were closed. The plaid blanket barely moved with his breath.

"Okay," Avery said quietly.

Eileen followed Avery out of the room. She closed the rolling door so the *Day Sleeper* sign showed.

Avery stood beside the warm kitchen stove. He held his hands spread open, close to the hot white enamel edge. His grandmother kissed him.

"He's very happy that you got to see him today," she said. She moved the big teapot onto the burner. "Will you stay for some tea or supper? I'll heat something up for you."

"No thanks. I should get home. I have homework."

She nodded and walked with him to the door. "You forgot to bring your book with you. Maybe tomorrow you can stop by after school and read some. I think Warren would like that."

"Okay," Avery opened the door and he stood on the step and touched the brass bell. He had to resist not giving the string a pull. "I'll see you tomorrow then."

She kissed him again and held him. "Thank you, Avery. We'll see you. Sweet dreams." She took a look at the yard and up the hill. "Be careful—it's getting dark."

"I will. Bye."

He forgot he was an airplane before. Now he was quiet in his thoughts, leaving the seashell path behind and Hickory Road and the rest of the way on dark Donovan home.

THURSDAY, October 18, 1962

VISION

He was quiet the rest of the night too. He watched a little TV, *The Jack Benny Show,* and when his mother got back from work, he went upstairs to sleep.

For a few hours he slept, until one o'clock, when the low rumbling from up Donovan began to approach. It sounded like the highway was making itself right down the street, inch by inch. When Avery awoke, he thought it was one of the logging trucks that groaned, shifting gears before dawn.

But this sound was a steady slow engine growl with red and yellow lights that swerved and lit the corners of his room. Avery hopped out of bed, grabbed his glasses and stumbled to the window, expecting to see the ground curling off like an apple peel.

The window pane hummed and shook. Avery pulled the curtains aside.

There was a house on the street. It was slowly being moved by two trucks, pushing and pulling it on a raft of timbers. The lights were flashing from the roofs of the trucks and there was one red beacon on the peak of the house. A few of the tree branches too close to the road bent and snapped off as it came through. The house continued past.

Avery knew that house from where the highway was going to plow through. It had lived there for years in a yard with pear trees and rose bushes. Now, in this last hour, it had picked up its moorings and left for high ground. It could have been on a river at night, the black flowing asphalt, the trees on either side, with a police car in its wake twirling blue lights.

It took fifteen minutes for the strange vision to float by. The rumble faded on up the hill, up beyond Hickory to a vacant lot waiting for it, a flat hollow where it would drop anchor and a new life would begin.

SHOCK

It wasn't a dream. When houses start getting up and walking, it's a sign. With the highway at the very edge of Donovan and readying to plow across, things were jumping. Roosting trees were toppled, favorite places for deer to settle in were gone, the football field too, Lockhart's Dairy was cut in half—the cows would have to dodge traffic to get to their pasture. Connelly Creek was a squashed pan of mud, the tractors were chewing and the concrete was moving in. Life was in retreat like a battlefield.

Just before lunch in Geometry class, Avery and everyone else in the room jumped at the sound of a distant explosion. Even the teacher froze, with a piece of chalk in his hand, an unfinished diagram on the blackboard. Tom Barters threw himself under his desk.

They stared at the eerie window in silence. Where was the flash? When would the shockwave bring smoke and glass shattering inside?

Mr. Hackett said, "Whatever that was, I don't think it was the Russians, Mr. Barters. Although I applaud your reflexes, I'm sure it's safe to return from your bomb shelter."

There was a nervous laughter as the boy reappeared.

The school bell clattered and soon the students were in the halls talking, in the lunch lines and out in the fenced yard, wondering what blew up. There were plenty of possibilities—a power plant, the Gull station, the refinery down south, the shipyard or cannery. It wasn't until after lunch, during the next class, when the principal spoke from the intercom.

"I know you've all been concerned about that loud noise we heard earlier. I just spoke with the deputy sheriff who informed me it came from the highway construction crew. To ensure safe passage of their new road, they found it necessary to dismantle Donovan Rock. Their operation was successful and I've been assured there won't be any further explosions to startle us. My thanks to staff and students for your patience."

The room was stunned. Even if you lived down State Street on the other side of town, everyone knew Donovan Rock. It was one of those things you took people from out of town to see. If the town had its own Wonders of the World, that huge Ice Age relic would have been on the list. The class sat there in shock like someone had been shot. Even the teacher had a hard time returning to the 18th Century. He stood by the board where he had written a word and he didn't know what to say.

Avery was used to that feeling. He touched the corner of his poetry book and thought of opening it to get away.

ALONE

While he read, the class moved on, the words from the front of the room became the sound of a motor pushing the room further away from him. Avery was left behind like a little floating island.

It wasn't until the last bell of the day, when the halls were full of everyone hurrying out, that Avery landed on earth again. It seemed like everyone was talking about the rock and half the school was walking out that way to see what happened. Avery was one of them too, crossing the wide lawn, hands thrust deep in his pockets, book under his arm. He walked shoulders hunched and eyes on the ground.

When he looked up, he wished he hadn't. He wished it had been a bad dream.

He saw Caroline on the corner holding hands with Kenny O'Donnell. They were off to see the rock like it was a picnic.

Avery slowed down and put his body against a tree, either to hide behind it, or to fall right in to that bark and become part of it. He watched her smile and laugh and they were talking so easily, crossing the street.

Avery ran his hand over the tree. He watched her float off with someone else.

He told himself that was okay. They could have the street, they could own the sunny Fall day and the birds in the trees too...No, he thought, and turned away. It's not okay.

It was one of those times you need Groucho Marx to enter and say something funny. If you couldn't laugh sometimes, it would seem like a cruel world.

Avery didn't want to see what happened to the stone anyway. What could he do about it now?

So he stood there beside the tree, knowing he had waited too long.

THE PATH

Instead of walking home on Donovan, he cut across the bridge and took the narrow path down into the gulley and the stream. There was a trail that ran in the bramble and ferns spilled down the hill towards the purl of water. There were a lot of branch-like shrubs that had lost their leaves for the winter, probably huckleberry. They brushed him going by. The stream level had gone down from what it was in the summer, but in another month there would be salmon returning to the rapids and pools.

The trail was muddy from the rains and Avery had to keep from sliding. There was devil's club, tall and spiny, that he didn't want to fall in, and a couple places he had to jump over washouts and ravines. The trail had been there a long time, mostly known by schoolboys, kept trampled by them for all these years, etched along the stream behind fields and backyards.

It was a good sound of running water and birds. Avery could think of other things. He could let his mind wander contently on the path; the smells of the fresh air and the forest all around him.

He went by the remains of an old car. All the glass was gone and the rusting metal shell of it stood out of the loam like an animal in a tar pit. There was an icebox, a broken washtub, stovepipe, the springs of a mattress, tin cans, a broken plow, rolled wire, and other tossed-away things. This had been the junkyard for a farm at one time. It made a strange scene for the stream to flow through. Some of the salmon may have been born among the smoothed broken bottles, a typewriter or radio parts.

There was a rope swing tied to a tall tree branch. You could swoop right over the incline, across the water and halfway up the ravine on the other side and then ride it with gaining speed back where you started.

Avery came out of the leaves to cross a road, then he went back into the brush. The deer must do this all the time. He looked for signs of them, but you could walk right by one and not even know it was there.

The cemetery was just through the trees and then he could see the Drive-In screen planked up against the sky. The path crept down closer to the creek and he searched the water for old movies junked in there. Was the Creature from the Black Lagoon asleep under that fallen tree? Did pirate's gold spill out of *Treasure Island* and glitter in a pool below? All those films that beamed over the field at night, surely something must fall off and sink forgotten into the wet leaves and stones?

BIRDS

He saw a small brown dipper bird dunk itself fearlessly in and out of the rapids. It climbed out onto a patch of sunlight blonde as Marilyn Monroe. It froze until Avery was gone.

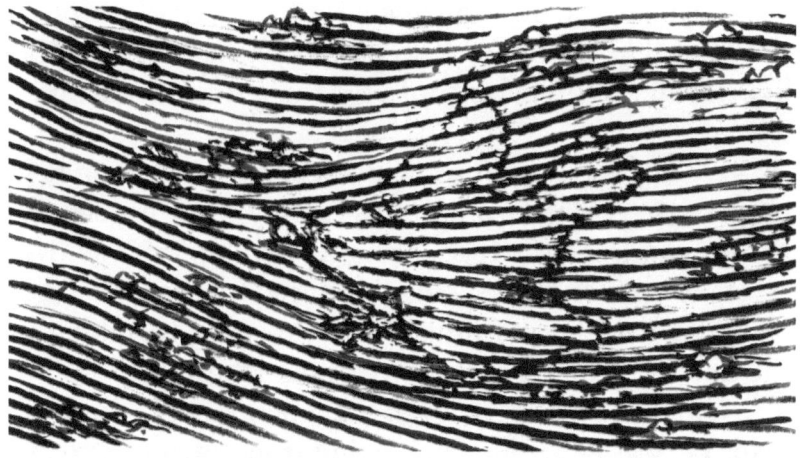

He would have liked to keep going, maybe follow the creek to where it became a bigger river joining colder water and hiking beside it as it roared, higher and higher to the snowy mountain beginnings.

The path branched away from the stream though. All those feet had trod beside it far enough and Avery was led out of the sound of running water and crunching leaves into the meadow grown around the Drive-In. The tall yellow weeds were folded where the deer passed through like canoes in the Sargasso Sea and Avery followed their route.

The storm damage had been repaired with 2x4 supports propped against the walls. They looked like the oars coming out of an ark. Splashing into the grass, they were pulling the theater until the wind could catch on the movie screens and it could sail free off the land, onto the bay. From there it could carry a cargo full of American late night fantasies overseas.

One time back in this field Avery startled a pheasant. It made a short loud flight away from him, dropping into a thicket fifty feet beyond. It left a colored blur in the air he could have reeled in like a long ribbon.

When he made it to the gravelly shoulder of Donovan, he made sure he didn't look for the rock as he crossed the road. Up in the blue sky flew a hawk, wings spread like out like a kite. You could see the red sunshine on its tail.

He had never seen so many people out walking here before. They weren't only the students from his school. Parked cars lined the road, bringing families from all over town. With everyone passing the Tweed Farm apple stand, he could have been selling cider. He could be raking in the dollars. People got thirsty coming all this way.

Crossing the street, Avery stepped straight into the field. He was being General, going from one place to another, finding the most peaceful place to be. He found it a little further on, where he climbed up into the crown of his favorite apple tree.

It used to take him a couple tries to swing up into the arms, now it was like getting on a horse. There was a knotted groove his foot fit in like a stirrup and he was settled high up in the nest.

DOWSING

A long time ago he carved his initials in the bark and there they were, worn as an old tattoo: *AT*.

With all that was going on, why was he sitting in a tree? It was calm. It slowed time. It turned everything into a photograph. He could see the orchard, smell the tart apple scented breeze, observe the way the field and fallen leaves quilted and readied the ground for winter. He didn't know what meditation was yet, but that's what it was. His hands rested folded on the cover of his book and he sat in his tree.

As he drifted along in his mind in his tree, across the orchard and up the hill, his thoughts stopped in the field where a memory lived.

There was his grandfather leading Avery around. It was summer and the trees were all bright green with sunshine and Avery held a dowsing stick, a Y-shaped twig Warren found for him. He told the boy the stick would tell him when water was underneath.

Avery walked round and round making a circular path in the grass, back to where his grandfather was waiting, watching him. There must be a trick to it, he thought. He held tight to the ends and closed his eyes and walked blindly, scanning the ground, wishing some electric signal would jump up from the water underground. He didn't feel anything.

But when his grandfather took the dowser, he didn't so much hold it as let it rest on his open hands like a bird, giving it a chance to fly when it wanted to and what do you know? In only a few steps, Avery watched the branch dip all by itself.

Avery felt sure he could do it now. He just wasn't so aware back then. Next time his grandfather could get out of bed, they could take a walk outside. It didn't have to be far. Avery just needed to find the right branch for dowsing and he could show his grandfather he knew about the invisible forces now.

When that memory left, Avery swung down from the tree, holding onto his book as he dropped. Soft moss grew like a dense forest and he continued on his way home, snapping twigs and leaving footprints. A woodpecker rattled a tree somewhere nearby.

STILL AROUND

Their house was waiting where it always was. No wheels or wings had taken it away during the day and Avery was happy to hop up the steps onto the porch. There were still cars on Donovan and some people walking and talking and he learned the next day that people were taking away pieces of the rock as souvenirs.

He turned the handle on the door and went inside. That's when something leaped and hit him in the legs.

Avery staggered and almost fell, but whatever it was in the dim hallway didn't mean him harm. It glowed like a paper lantern and it wagged its tail and barked.

"Gizmo!"

Avery kneeled and held out his arms and the full pillowy force of his ghostly dog hit him again. Avery wrapped his arms around his pet and squeezed. There was enough substance that his arms did not pass entirely through. It was like hugging a dog made of cloth.

"I knew you were still around!" Avery laughed as the dog danced around the hallway, skittering on the wooden floor like he used to. But he wasn't quite the same as he was when he was alive—he was almost see-through, like a smudge. Also, he sort of glowed, like one of those white or yellow opal stones you could find on the beach. When you held it up to the sun that light fuzzed right through the rock. "Come here, Gizmo!"

The ghost dog jumped back in his arms and Avery stood up holding him. It did occur to him to wonder what his mother would say. She seemed to like not having a dog anymore and here he was returned from the grave and who knows for how long?

Avery carried his dog to the living room and sat on the couch with him. Gizmo still had his corner with a new pillow now for him to lie on. Avery couldn't let him go though. He buried his face in that vapor and fur. After all that happened today, finally something good...Losing Gizmo last year had been awful. He felt like he had been made lonely, but now it was just a bad dream.

"I don't know where you were or how long you can stay, but I'm sure glad you came back."

For a long time Avery sat there petting the dog as the house slipped quietly into evening. When he asked, "Are you hungry? You want dinner?" he expected that old look from his pet. Those words used to send Gizmo scampering ahead of him. But the dog looked quite content. "Yeah, you're a ghost. You probably don't need to eat, do you?" He stood up. "Anyway, I do."

He went to the kitchen and the dog followed. Avery heated up some leftovers and sat at the formica table with his poetry book.

Gizmo still watched him eat, head tipped, but when Avery tried to share, the dog wasn't interested.

"No food in heaven, huh?" Or maybe there was, he thought. Maybe everything was so good, there was no need for earthly things again—except for seeing old friends separated by that cloudy space. "Did you come all the way back to see me?" Avery asked. "There's a story in my book about that. I should have named you Orpheus." Gizmo was his grandfather's name for the dog because the puppy acted like a little toy robot.

Avery finished his dinner. He washed the dishes. They returned to the living room and watched TV and Avery pet Gizmo and really began to wonder what he could say to his mother when she got home.

Gizmo was easier to care for. No more shedding fur or buying bags of dog food. He might not even carry shoes around the house the way he used to. His mouth would probably pass right through. There was no reason he couldn't stay with them, was there?

COAL

They were watching *The Many Loves of Dobie Gillis* when the car arrived. The door slammed. Gizmo jumped off Avery's lap and ran into the hall. "Oh boy!" Avery said, "Here we go."

Gizmo's feet skittered on his claws as he jumped around beside the front door. He gave a nervous bark as the handle turned, as she opened the door and stepped right through the bounding dog.

She laughed, "It's just me, Avery."

Gizmo passed back and forth through her legs barking, unseen and unheard and unfelt by her.

"What's the matter?" she said. "Is Grandpa okay?"

Avery realized he must be standing there like a ghost himself. "No...I'm okay."

"You look like I let Peter Lorre in behind me." She turned around and looked to be sure before she shut the door.

Gizmo ran past Avery who felt the dog brush him, clattering into the kitchen and into the living room. What was going on? Why couldn't she see their dog?

She hung up her coat on the wall, said how cold it was getting outside, and did he see what they did to the rock? It was terrible. She kissed Avery as she made her way to the kitchen and never noticed the dog still racing about.

"Well," said Avery. "I think I'll go to sleep." If he was in *The Twilight Zone*, that seemed like the safest thing to do.

Gizmo saw him go and ran up the stairs ahead of him. Wasn't it just like the old days? Only now there was a ghost waiting at the foot of Avery's bed.

"I knew you always understood me," Avery said. "I wish you could say what's going on though."

He got undressed and got in bed. Gizmo stepped over his stretched feet and settled between Avery's legs and the wall. That used to be like having a warm coal beside him.

FRIDAY, October 19, 1962

SPELLBOUND

It took a dream that night to figure it out. Avery was on the blacktop of Donovan Ave, looking at the rock. It was still big as a house in the middle of the road. It was painted with that bear paw.

And so, as Avery stood on the edge of the road, planted like a tree, he watched while the rock began to crack. Even in his dream it reminded him of a movie, when the dinosaur egg breaks open and the person seeing it happen is spellbound and frozen.

Avery saw the pieces splinter and fall as from the middle of the rock an enormous brown bear emerged. It knocked great chunks of stone aside with its claws. The bear raised its head to sniff the air and give the street a stare.

Avery hoped he was invisible as the bear began to lumber down Donovan towards him.

Then it stopped and swiped a paw off the ground like a painter's brush. Huge, old-growth fir trees sprung from Lockhart's dairy field. The bear created another dense forest on the other side of the road. The sunlight in Avery's dream was being shaded away.

The bear took another few steps closer. This time it swung its paw at the Bayview Cemetery which was across the tar from Avery. Suddenly, from out of the plots and around the grave marker stones, the ghosts of people appeared. The lawn was filled with them. They were all sizes, all ages, and some of them were dressed from another century. There must be a lot of dead people waiting on the other side. Avery knew if he kept looking he would see his father and brother.

But the bear made the thick forest grow again. Within them hid the ghost animals, deer and birds and a mountain lion. As the bear stalked along the road it was bringing back another world.

It was so close the bear could have stretched out and snapped up Avery whole in one bite. It did give him a look as it rumbled by. There was moss growing in the big footprints. It left a shining wake that covered the road. It reminded Avery of the side street downtown, unused for so long it was turning green again. The iron breath of the beast chuffed by like an old fashioned steam engine train and as it left down Donovan, making ghosts along the way, from out of the ruins of the rock, riding on the smooth sea-green moss, appeared a cedar canoe. It paddled out, followed by another and another. They were just like the sepia photos Avery saw at the museum. They paddled, dipped into the Donovan stream. A man in a straw hat looked right at Avery and the sound of those ghost Salish canoes made a rhythmic chuff, chuff, chuff as they passed. Then Avery had his eyes open, looking at his darkened room.

Gizmo was dreaming too, breathing in choppy almost barks, his paws were clawing at the wall. It was like the sound of those canoes cutting through the blacktop turning into water.

Were there more ghosts out there? Did other people see them? Would the whole town be walking around with ghosts tomorrow?

Avery stuck his arm out of the covers to pet the dog. His hand went into a gray soft bunched knot of blanket at the foot of his bed. It wasn't his old ghostly dog.

Avery sat up. It was just him in the room.

The clock dial glowed 3:29.

He heard a train horn away in the early morning. When it was gone, the room became that empty, hungry quiet again. He lay back down. It wasn't entirely quiet. He heard a breeze go by in the leaves. Or maybe it was a car. He closed his eyes. The clock ticked.

It was funny that he hadn't noticed the clock before. That contraption never stopped. Unless he forgot to wind it, it would tick and tock forever, or at least until he wasn't around anymore. He knew he only had a few more hours to sleep. Across the sloped curve of the globe, the sun was moving out of the cold Atlantic Ocean, headed this way. He yawned and felt with his feet for Gizmo, touching only the wall.

TREASURE

It seemed like he only closed his eyes for a second. Then it was breakfast and his mother had the radio on and she was telling him about the rock. "They dug five holes, ten feet deep around it, stuffed with twelve pounds of dynamite. Can you believe that? They made a bomb out of it!"

Avery couldn't believe it. He didn't want to believe it. When he went outside to get the bus he made sure he didn't look that way. And when he took his seat, he tried not to listen. At school he tried to tune out the frequency of anyone talking about the rock or anyone who might have brought a piece of it to show. He didn't want to know.

And that wasn't all—there was also the dance. The intercom buzzed with the news of it twice during the day and there were painted signs in the hallways and the gym was being decorated with crepe streamers everywhere. Everything reminded him that Caroline would be there with someone else.

He was just trying to make it through the day, head down, arm around his book, when Tony caught him before the next class bell.

"Avery, I need your help tonight." He saw the pained look on Avery's face. "Don't worry. It's not about rockets. This is way bigger than rockets. You won't believe it."

"What is it?"

"I can't tell you. No—listen! This is something you need to see to believe."

Avery rolled his eyes. They were talking next to a banner for the dance and he winced from that sight.

Tony's voice dropped, "Do the words *buried treasure* mean anything to you?"

Avery was about to answer but Tony hushed him.

A girl stopped at the drinking fountain below the dance poster. She held her ponytail from getting wet.

Tony said, "We'll pick you up tonight."

"We?"

"Yeah. Jerry's driving."

Avery stared at him. "Jerry! I thought his car was wrecked?"

Tony shrugged. "His dad's a car salesman. He gave him another one off the lot."

"I don't know. That was pretty crazy last time he drove."

"We won't do anything crazy this time. Believe me, you don't want to miss it."

"Buried treasure?"

"Shhh!"

Avery switched the big book to his other arm. It had to be better than sitting at home, fretting about the dance, or the rock. "What time?"

"Seven." Tony smiled. "We'll pick you up."

The bell rang and they started to part. The waxy floor squeaked with shoes hurrying for class.

"Oh!" Tony called over his shoulder. "You need to bring a shovel!" He waved and was gone into a room before Avery could reply.

DAYDREAM

At least that gave Avery something to think about during the last class. Of course he took notes but his mind was really floating forward in time to the evening. *A shovel?* Why did he need a shovel? Where were they digging? How could Jerry be driving them again? His father just handed out cars like the gumball machine at the pharmacy. *Buried treasure?* That made Avery think of the cemetery...It better not be there—I'm not digging up a grave, he thought, sketching a ghost floating over his notes.

Avery's handwriting, already small and bunched tight letters, became little shoals and waves and the shapes of islands. He drew a sailing ship riding atop the longest word. He made sails full of wind and flying from the tallest mast was a pirate flag. On deck, he drew a tiny captain stick figure with a peg leg. With the pencil lead waiting beside it, Avery imagined this was no ordinary pirate—he took his peg leg from the carved leg of a grand piano. He was Piano Leg! He was known and feared across the seven seas. He even had a piano on deck that he would play while the battle raged. The sound of Beethoven drifting out over the waves in the fog, played by a hand and a silver hook, would be your only warning that Piano Leg was nearby. And try as they might, the combined navies of the world could never catch Piano Leg. Avery drew the island where the infamous pirate lived. Surrounded in coral reef and fog, Avery turned some letters into palm trees. There, on the peak of the extinct volcano, with a view of the whole world around him, Piano Leg played his haunting solid gold piano.

"Mr. Tweed?"

Avery was thrown on the shore of the classroom, his daydream shipwrecked.

"Mr. Tweed, before we all leave for the weekend, could you share your answer with us?" Mrs. Bartlett and everyone in class watched him under the spotlight.

Avery glanced at his notes. They told a whole other story he didn't think they would want to hear. "Well..." he began. He pushed his glasses. He looked at the window. Even the trees were waiting, tall dark green firs the crows liked to land atop. Well, he thought. His mind was racing. He thought of Jack Benny, holding his hand to his face in that mocked surprise that would always make the audience laugh.

The bell rang.

Mrs. Bartlett spoke through the sound of it. "It seems that Mr. Tweed has been quite literally saved by the bell."

There was a flurry of books closing, paper shuffling and movement—coats going on and the crinoline sound of skirts and dresses. Avery hastily grabbed his poetry book. He thought one last time of Piano Leg, running the gauntlet, fleeing before the King of England's flagship, making for open water. When he made it through the doorway, out into the hallway, he knew he got away.

As he hurried down the stone steps onto the sidewalk, he would have become an airplane or rocket if he was still in grade school. It was still tempting to think about. All it took was the sight of Caroline to crash that thought. She was on her way home to dress for the dance. He could picture her there, in the gym tonight with the music and colored lights, looking like Cinderella. Avery got on his bus, found a seat by the window and opened up his book.

PAGES

He didn't really feel like reading though. He placed his hands on either page the way he had seen his grandfather dowse. He tried to read it by reaching beyond. The bus started to move. The big book was a river stone. Words poured in a current over it. How many times had he sat by the creek, mesmerized by the silvery flow? He thought a book like this could be made into a long river, pages laid out like white choppy water in a line from school to home, the path he took every day.

The school bus went over the bridge above Padden's green creek, slowed and took a right turn onto Donovan. Avery thought of Perry Roberts on the corner sowing the rapids with the pages of his own poetry. Avery was sure there were other people he had never met—they were standing along the banks too—and the poets nobody knew were adding more pages as the bus went rushing by. Past the cemetery and the Drive-In, up the side of the hill the pages climbed, by Highland and then Hickory.

Avery turned to catch sight of his grandparents' house. It looked quiet, like a fairytale cabin in the wood. I'll go see them tomorrow, thought Avery. The pages were running out. Now it was Dylan Thomas finishing up as the watery pages ran thin as a trickle in the valley and the bus slowed to a stop at the nearly dry ditch by the Tweed Farm sign.

Avery closed his book. It found his house. He could see it through the autumn leaves.

When he got off the bus, he still didn't have the heart to look to his right to see what remained of the rock. Sooner or later, he knew he would, but not now. He crossed the street and made a jump onto the seashells.

GHOST

His mother had left the red wheelbarrow waiting for him. It was parked in the driveway without any white chickens or glazed with rain, still it made him think of William Carlos Williams. Avery took hold of the wooden handles. It was up to him to roll it through the fields, to fill it with apples, to crush in the press to make cider to sell by the road.

So that's what he did with the rest of the daylight. He felt surrounded by the years others worked the land, all the truck farms around their orchard, gathering their produce—carrots, cabbage and lettuce, cherries, blueberries, beans and strawberries—to drive into town, up and down the neighborhood alleys, or filling a wheelbarrow to push and sell. By the time he parked the wheelbarrow, it was heavy with fruit and the sun was burrowing into the hill. There was no noise coming from the highway. If there were any ghosts in canoes, or any lost souls from the cemetery, Avery didn't notice. The valley seemed to be pulling over shadows and going to sleep.

Before he went inside, Avery remembered to get a shovel. He stood it on the porch, leaning against the pillar like a witch's broom.

Opening the door, he held his breath, hoping Gizmo would be there. But it was just a quiet hallway and, as he took a breath, the same old familiar smell. Whatever disturbance caused by Donovan Rock blowing up must have spread out and moved on, the way a dropped stone will leave disappearing ripples on the surface of a pond.

Avery hung up his coat and carried his book to the kitchen. He pictured himself as a ghost, living in this old farmhouse, surrounded by apple trees in a valley that was modernizing fast and about to disintegrate with the arrival of the highway that would soon be rumbling with gigantic trucks bringing food the little farms couldn't compete with and the pastures and orchards would be turned by bulldozers into lots for houses, vanishing into the night.

Avery ate a sandwich and creaked on the floor and sat on the sofa and laughed at black and white comedians on TV and when there were headlights in the driveway and the bleat of a horn, he jumped up.

SHOVEL

They were in a station wagon this time. Tony held an arm out the window, waving as Avery came down the steps with his shovel. Tony turned his open wave into a thumb pointing, "Hop in."

Avery opened the heavy passenger door and slid onto the vinyl seat. He slanted the shovel next to him.

Jerry had the radio going, giving the steering wheel a drumbeat before he put the car back in gear.

The yard swerved in the beams of white light and Avery asked, "We're not going too far, are we?" He didn't want another speed trial, or game of chase.

Tony said, "Not far at all. My dad's apartment."

"We're digging for treasure in your dad's apartment?"

"The yard next door to it."

Avery saw a light on in his grandparents' house. It made a lonely sight. He hoped they were alright. He remembered he promised he would read poetry there.

Jerry floored the gas pedal so the station wagon roared on the hill.

Avery held the back of the seat tightly as they topped Highland and began down the other side. Over at the Moonlite, cars were starting to line up. It was Friday night and *King Solomon's Mines* was playing. Across the bridge, pretty soon cars would be arriving for the dance in the gym. There were so many things to do and here he was, in the backseat of a station wagon, holding a shovel. Was there any justice in the world?

Avery rolled down his window. The car braked, the tires squealed as they took a sharp turn. He saw a pumpkin glowing on a porch. Halloween was only a week away.

South Hill crept around them. Avery was glad the narrow neighborhood streets slowed them down. He noticed more pumpkins, orange lanterns here and there.

One house had three of them in the window. Some of the houses they passed were like palaces. Shining with electricity, they looked out at the bay. Way out, seen from a boat, they must look like stars.

Avery remembered the little greenish light on his grandparents' house…The lamp on the kitchen table… Enough to draw a hungry moth to the window.

"Hey, Jerry," Tony said. "Tell Avery your TV commercial idea for your dad's car lot."

Jerry turned down another twist song on the radio, "You know that show, *Mister Ed*? With the talking horse?"

Of course Avery knew it. He didn't like it though. They pulled the horse's lip with fishing line to make it speak. He could imagine what General would think of that.

"Mister Edsel!" Jerry said. "The camera focuses on the grill of an Edsel while it tells what all the best deals on the lot are!"

"Get it?" Tony said.

Avery shrugged, "I guess so. It's a talking car."

"Named Mister Edsel! It's a pun!" Jerry explained.

Rolling eyes don't make any sound. The atmosphere was silent and Avery held onto the shovel as the car coasted against the curb and Jerry shut off the motor. The music went with it. Quiet.

Tony and Avery left the car and waited on the narrow swath of grass beside the sidewalk while Jerry sat behind the wheel, sullenly lighting a cigarette.

"Where's Harold?" Avery asked.

Tony poked his shoe at the lumpy grass. "He got grounded. He can't go out again until his cast comes off."

They watched a puff of smoke escape the driver's side window.

Avery said, "Sorry. I didn't know he was so touchy about Mister Ed."

"You just have to humor him."

Avery tapped the ground with the shovel. "Where's the treasure?"

Tony tipped his head and half whispered, "The backyard of that house."

"The backyard?"

"Shh!"

"I don't want to dig in someone's backyard."

"Relax, Avery. I've got it all figured out. I've been watching from my dad's apartment. I've seen this guy burying treasure. All we have to do is sneak back there and get it."

"And what if the guy sees us?"

"He won't. He's never around at this time. He goes to the Drive-In. My dad says he goes there every night."

Avery gave the grass a little chop with the blade.

"Don't worry. I know the spot. It will only take a minute."

"What kind of treasure?"

"I don't know exactly. Gold coins or something... He's one of those kooky old guys who buries things in the backyard."

"Well, we should get this over with. It looks pretty weird standing around with a shovel. Is Jerry our getaway driver?"

"I don't know what's taking him. I think he's steamed. You didn't like his commercial."

Avery shook his head in disbelief.

"I kid you not. Jerry's kind of sensitive. Look—here he comes."

MOONLIGHT

Jerry stood beside the car and gave one last draw on his cigarette, then flicked it into the street. He shut the door and walked around the front of the station wagon. When he stepped onto the curb beside Avery and Tony, he exhaled the cloud he'd been holding. He laughed and coughed, "Looks like you're waiting to go grave digging with Count Misfit."

"Well, come on then," Tony said. "Follow me." He took them across the sidewalk, along the wooden fence that bordered the apartment building. They had to duck below some branches and then they were behind the fence, in the neighbor's yard.

There were a couple squares of yellow light cast from the apartment windows, laid down like carpet on the dark grass. They avoided those patches as they ran across the lawn.

Tony stopped at the edge of a garden, a bird fountain and flat stones surrounded by shrubs. He got down on a knee and examined the soil. He looked back up at Jerry and Avery and whispered, "This is the spot."

Avery was staring back across the lawn at the dark house, the big screened porch and the two windows above it on the second floor that looked like eyes watching him in its yard.

Jerry gave Avery's shoulder a rough push. "You heard him, dig!"

Avery pressed the point of the shovel on the dirt and hopped on the dull top of the blade. It sunk in easily and he leaned on it and scooped up a pile of earth. He spread it out and Tony searched it for gold.

"Try it again," Tony said.

There was nothing like the eerie sound of a shovel at night. Avery had the terrible feeling that any second they would be caught.

"Wait!" Tony brushed the dirt off his opened palm. He held a couple smooth white stones.

Jerry bent down and stared, "They're just rocks!"

Still, Avery could have sworn they were something. He reached out a hand to hold one just as a ray, brighter than moonlight, swept across the lawn into the driveway.

CAUGHT

An old black car rattled on the stones and stopped in front of the closed door of the carriage house.

"Run!" Jerry shouted as he snapped like elastic. Tony bumped against Avery, bolting after Jerry.

For a long moment Avery continued to stand there with his shovel, watching the car, headlights dim, hearing the motor cough off, seeing the driver open the squeaking door. Then he ran.

He ran with the shovel held out in front of him like some silent movie comedian on the go. He didn't seem to know he was carrying such an absurd prop as he crashed into the lilac tree and hit the fence. There was no way he could pass through the narrow gap between the boards the way Tony and Jerry had escaped. Old wood splintered, branches snapped, Avery rebounded and fell into a rose bush.

Avery tried to stand but fell in deeper. His glasses were snatched off. The thorns were ripping his jacket, his jeans and tearing his skin. He still held the shovel across him like a paddle. Could he use it to leverage himself out?

"Hold on there. Let me take that shovel out of your way."

Avery saw an old man and let him help. The rose bush crunched and pierced as he moved. He tried not to cry out.

The old man sat the shovel on the lawn and offered his hands. "Let's see if we can get you out of there."

There was a lot of snapping and Avery could feel branches hook into him, breaking off the bush.

"That was some departure," the old man said after Avery could stand.

"Sorry about your rose. I didn't mean to do that." He picked up his glasses beside a broken limb.

"I know."

Avery wiped his face with the back of his hand and stared at the blood.

"Looks like my rose should be apologizing to you. We better get those cuts taken care of."

Avery could feel the sting of them now. It felt like the time he stepped on a beehive.

The old man passed him his shovel. "Come on inside."

"Is that your house?"

"It sure is."

"I'm sorry we were in your backyard. I didn't want to make any trouble." Avery limped along beside the old man.

Avery blinked and rubbed his brow with the sleeve of his coat. It was too dark to see if it was blood or shadow.

KITCHEN

The old man opened the porch door and held it for Avery. "You can set your trusty weapon against the rocking chair. We'll go in to the kitchen. I'll get my first aid kit."

"Thanks."

The old man turned on the kitchen light. He pointed to a table. There was an old overturned top hat with a glass vase set inside of it. A fresh bunch of tropical flowers popped out of it. They looked all around the kitchen.

On the wall by the fridge, Avery saw a poster for the circus. It had a blue elephant in a ring. There was an old newspaper clipping in a little frame below it. Avery read the headlines, *Elephant Still AWOL*.

The old man seemed to be younger than Avery thought out in the dark. Maybe it was just the clothes he wore that made him look old.

"Have a seat," he told Avery. "I'll be right back."

There were red scratches all over Avery's hands. He sat down but kept his hands in the air, off the tablecloth. He looked around a little more. He liked the kitchen. A big teapot on the stove like his grandmother used, a pyramid of tea boxes and tins stacked on a shelf. Some had Japanese or Chinese writing. On the windowsill above the table was a clay bowl with a sort of Mayan design. Avery guessed that's what it was. He spent a lot of time in his grandparents' house reading their old 1940 encyclopedia set.

There was a *Herald* folded in half on the table in front of him. The crossword was complete. There was an empty cup beside the paper.

Avery was looking at the photograph of a sailboat framed on the yellow painted wall—two boys looked out of the picture at him—when the old man returned with his first aid. He had a box of bandaids, a bag of cotton and a small bottle. He ran the water in the sink and waited for it to get warm. "That's good," he said and he filled a big porcelain serving bowl with soapy water and brought it to the table. "Wash your arms and face with this." There was a washcloth floating on the surface like a lily pad.

Avery dipped his hands in. They stung squeezing the cloth and it stung his face and arms too, but it did feel better.

The old man turned on the stove burner and came back with a towel which he passed to Avery. He also had a mirror that he leaned against the wall.

"Thanks."

"Daub some of that on the cotton and wipe your scratches."

"Okay." Avery watched himself in the mirror as he prepared the cotton and made a face, waiting for it to hurt as he pressed it on his forehead. He was surprised when it didn't. The hydrogen peroxide they used at home let you know when it went on.

The old man was fixing two cups of cocoa. The big kettle gave a wheeze as he moved it off the stove and poured hot water in with some milk and powdered chocolate. "My name's Robert Canfield."

"I'm Avery. Avery Tweed."

Robert returned to the table with the two cups.

"Pleased to meet you, Avery."

The way he said it almost got Avery to laugh he was so relieved.

Robert pushed a cup towards Avery. "Are you thirsty?"

"Sure. Thank you." Avery's hands were full.

"Oh, you can throw that cotton away under the sink."

Avery carried the ball of cotton to the sink and tossed it in the garbage behind the cupboard door.

"Well, you look better now. Help yourself to those bandaids though."

"We were looking for treasure," Avery said. He stuck a couple bandages on his hands.

Robert took a sip. "Did you find any?"

"A couple white stones." He felt bad. Avery stared at his cocoa. It had little islands of bubbles.

Robert chuckled. "You found the treasure then." He took another sip and asked, "Did you see me bury them there?"

Avery shook his head. "I didn't. Someone I know from school. I think I was only along because I have a shovel."

Robert smiled. He didn't seem angry at all. Maybe it happened all the time.

Avery said, "I can get them back for you."

"That's okay. They lost their power. They only work if they stay underground."

"They're magic?"

Robert nodded.

They both had some cocoa and thought about it.

"What kind of magic?" Avery asked. It was easy for

him to believe in things.

"They were for protection."

"For you?"

Robert smiled. "No." He stood up and walked towards the refrigerator. "They're for the Kennedys."

"The President?"

"And his brother, the Attorney General..." Robert took a clipping off the fridge and returned to the table with it. "This is from last August." His eyes squinted as he read, *"Seattle—Rest and relaxation were uppermost in the mind of U.S. Attorney General Robert F. Kennedy Monday night as he arrived for a brief stay in this World Fair city."* Robert paused and looked at Avery, "I was there the next day at the Playhouse for his speech. Listen to this..." He unfolded the next article taped to the back, *"We must strive day and night to devise the machinery which will limit and eventually abolish national arms and destroy forever the means and opportunities of aggression."* Robert stared at the words a moment. He was back there again. He stood in a long line. He could see Kennedy ahead of him, nodding and smiling and moving. He could see the Space Needle rocketing up at the sky. He could feel the excitement of being there, being one of the lucky people to be there. "You can see why he might need some protection, right? Well, I held the stone in hand the whole time he spoke. I made sure the magic would hold. These stones have the power to save lives, to keep a person from danger, but only if they're charged when you're nearby. You have to be in the near vicinity." He brought the cup up for a drink. "Later on, I saw the President when he came to Seattle last winter. He gave a speech at the university and I was there with another stone." He set his empty cup down.

"So I had those two Kennedy stones since August. I kept them together right there in that dish on the windowsill. Maybe if I would have kept them a little longer, or buried them right away, nobody would have seen me bury them." He shrugged. For a second he looked as old as Avery's grandfather.

Avery said, "The Kennedys will come back though, won't they?"

"Of course. I'm sure they will. I'll just have to start over. I keep an eye on the newspaper. In fact, I read that the President will be headed back this way soon."

STONES

"Where did you get the stones?"

"Oh, I found those on the beach. Sometimes I find them in streams or rivers, sometimes in the woods. I've found them in town too, in a vacant lot, or when I'm gardening. It makes me wonder if people put them there a long time ago and I'm just finding them again."

"Yeah, maybe," Avery said.

"But I found the Kennedy stones on Poe's Point."

"That's where we go to get seashells. Maybe I could meet you there sometime to find some new stones? I feel I owe it to you. You could teach me how to find them."

"Okay," Robert smiled. "We can try."

Then it occurred to Avery, "What if we don't find new stones? Will the Kennedys die?"

"The world has lots of ways of playing itself out. There's always more than one way reality can go. We're in this one now, but who knows the direction it will take to become something new? That's why we have to do whatever it takes to protect the good things around us."

"Are you sure they work? Have you tried them before?"

"So far so good. Of course nobody lasts forever. I've just found that these stones make life last a little longer and for someone you care about, that means a great deal. Like I said, you do what you can." Robert wrapped his fingers around his empty cup. "Anyway, I better let you go back to your friends. They're probably thinking the worst."

Avery stood up, "Thanks for the cocoa."

"You're welcome, Avery." He stood up from the table too. He laughed, "Just think, if I decided to stay at the Moonlite tonight, we never would have met. And I wouldn't have known the Kennedy stones were gone.

Who knows how history could have changed from this night?"

"That's true."

"Oh, before you go," Robert crossed the floor to the window and reached into the Mayan bowl on the ledge. "Would you like to have this stone?" It was a reddish round rock, the size of a radish. He put it on Avery's open hand.

"Is this magic?"

"It will be when you charge it. You just think of someone you care about...Someone nearby to you. Then put it in the ground or in a lake or the ocean, somewhere it won't be found."

"Thank you, Mr. Canfield."

He nodded. "You stop by again sometime and we'll go to Poe's Point. I have a feeling we'll find a couple new Kennedy stones."

Avery left the kitchen and got his shovel and when he left the porch, he turned around. "Thanks for not being angry."

Robert Canfield waved from the porch.

"I'll see you." Avery carried his shovel and as he glanced at the garden he wondered how many other stones were buried under there. How many other people owed their life to magic spells?

REALITIES

Avery walked out of the neighborhood, out of the shadows of trees and porches, onto the cement sidewalk of State Street. He knew it must look weird, a kid carrying a shovel on a busy road lined by bars and neon and the piercing lights of cars.

When he left Robert Canfield's yard there was no sign of Jerry's car. Avery figured he and Tony must have deserted him in their hurry to escape. It would have been a long walk home, back across South Hill to his house, so Avery walked the other way, to where his mother would be working, nearly done with her shift at the bowling alley.

It was Friday night and the jukeboxes were spilling from open doors. He knew it was the music of the day, but he still kept his radio dial on the big band orchestras, crooners and torch songs.

Someone greeted Avery as Johnny Appleseed and someone else laughed at the joke. He tried to hold the shovel hidden tight against his side like a crutch.

When the Star Lanes neon marquee sign started to appear, Avery watched for an opening in the traffic so he could cross the wide street. The blocks were far apart and there wasn't a crosswalk until the stoplight on Forest Street.

He thought he saw Jerry's station wagon but it was filled with people from his school—boys in suits and girls in dresses. The dance was probably still going on. Avery thought about the different realities Robert Canfield spoke of and how in one of them Caroline must be holding some luckier version of him, with her head on his shoulder and he could smell her hair. Avery sighed. That was a dream world, far away from this one where he carried a shovel along a lonely city street, covered in scratches.

He slipped in between two parked cars when he saw the street was clear and made a run for it. It felt like he was in the trough of the town, the seam run by cars and trucks and taxis. The streetcars weren't around anymore but you could feel them in that wind rushing to get from one place to another.

ROLLING

The sidewalk on the other side was made of orangey window light from the Pizza and Pipes restaurant. They were open late. Coming through the glass, you could hear the big pipe organ shaking like Captain Nemo in a sinking submarine and past all the tables, Avery could see Laurel & Hardy projected on the wall. In front of them was the tallest stairway and they had to get a piano up it.

Avery walked by the letters on the frosty glass. In front of him the tilted Star Lanes sign shined in the sky. He was starting to read all the words around him as lines in poetry.

There was a thin lane that ran between the pizza parlor and the bowling alley, a sort of crease in the map, and in that space stood Perry Roberts. He wavered in the feeble light that reached him as if he was not quite a part of the landscape. As Avery slowed in recognition, Perry swiveled on a heel and faced him. "Aha!" he called out. "If it isn't young Robinson Jeffers..."

"No, sir. I'm Avery Tweed."

"Of course you are. Have you seen the sea tonight, Mr. Tweed?" His arms raised and he swayed at the narrow sight of the sparkling black bay. And then he cleared his throat and said in a long and sonorous flow, "By the sea that was lying down still and green as grass after a night of tar-black howling and rolling, I went out of the house, where I had come to stay for a cold unseasonable holiday." Perry may have forgotten Avery was there. As he recited he moved towards that water, further into the gloom between the walls, arms held out wide like a marionette.

Avery wanted to tell Perry Roberts about the poetry books but Perry was drifting off with the night. Avery supposed Perry Roberts would go find poetry washed ashore among the white shells, the mussels and the magic stones, and when he woke up like driftwood, Dallas Clay would be there to help the poet to his feet and guide him ashore. The voice carried off and Avery could hear the faint roar of the bowling lanes broadcast from the ventilation slats.

So Avery turned from the alley telescoping off to the sea, and he rounded the corner to join the light of the Star Lanes blinking marquee.

SONG

A loud city bus went by on the street.

Avery opened the Star Lanes door and carried the shovel in. He hopped up a couple steps and he could see all the lanes to his right, stretched out in gold waxy rows.

The place was crowded with bowlers and people on plastic chairs, laughing, talking, cheering. Dance music was blasting out the speakers. The pinball machines were lit and clanging.

He saw his mother carrying a tray between tables at the end of the long shoe rental counter. He kept walking straight through towards the grill and the cluster of tables around it. That was also where The Ripper spun his records in a little booth. Avery recognized the song that began to play as he made his way there.

With Ricky Nelson left singing "A Traveling Man," The Ripper opened the gate and walked towards Avery. He wore black sunglasses and a Hawaiian shirt, raising his hand in salute.

Avery couldn't even see his eyes but he waved back as he sat at a table by the wall. He rested the shovel beside him.

"Avery. Long time no see." Then The Ripper stopped and tipped his dark glasses down his nose, noticing the shovel and the scratches. "What happened to you? You get in a fight with a rake?"

"Oh...It's a long story."

"I bet. You were supposed to be at the school dance tonight."

"I know. I should have been." Avery must have looked pretty pathetic. He stared at the torn sleeve of his coat, the scratches on the back of his hand and the bandaids. He thought of other realities again.

"Well, I think I've got the song for you. You just sit tight."

There was so much sound in the place Avery felt like he was riding on a big lily pad of noise.

Bowling balls rolling, crashing pins, yells and clatters and Ricky Nelson fading away around the globe.

The Ripper let the song go to just that point where it could barely be heard and the next song began with a vinyl crackle. There were heartbreak songs Avery heard on the radio in his room, those 1940s wartime orchestras had plenty to be blue about, but they seemed to grow them by the acres for teenagers today. They got played a few times and tossed aside to make room for the next one on the chart. It was the world's largest junkyard of broken hearts.

And as Avery listened to the song begin, he was pulled right in from the first, by that rusted, battered saxophone, the drumbeat thump, piano and guitar line, and then when Barbara Lynn sang, "If you should lose me," something happened. It was just the way he felt—that saxophone dragging itself, the piano, the guitar spangling and sliding and the heart thumping drum. "If you lose me," she sang, "Oh yeah, you lose a good thing."

Avery forgot about his Friday night date with a shovel. He found the stone Robert gave him and he made a prayer for Caroline. They were in the same town. The magic would work. Even if they weren't together, they were close. When Avery was done, and as the slow song began to end, he put the stone back in his coat pocket.

RELIEF

He was back in the bowling alley. There was a new song on the record player and he could see his mother returning from the tables with an empty orange tray. As the bright lights from the ceiling caught her glasses and made them shine, she noticed Avery. Her mouth went open and he could almost hear her gasp above the noise.

"Avery!" she said when she reached him five seconds later. "What are you doing here? What happened to you?" She brushed his face with her free hand.

"I goofed," he said.

"Is that our shovel?"

He explained, "It turns out darkness is not the best time to go treasure hunting."

"Look at you! Look at your new coat!"

"It's not that new."

"Oh, Avery..." She patted the torn sleeve. "I'll be done in ten minutes if you want a ride home. Unless you're looking to get into more trouble?"

"No, mom."

She shook her head. "You want me to order you some food?"

He looked at the grill. The cook had a couple hamburgers sizzling. "Maybe...I don't know. Can we get something to bring home? I think I'd like to wait in the car if that's okay."

"Alright." She took the keys out of her apron. "I'll be there soon."

She kissed him and carried her tray away. She looked pretty tired too. It was a long shift going back and forth. It's too bad, he thought, we can't just make our living on the farm.

Avery stood and took his shovel. He saw a man in a purple team jacket throw his arms in the air and roar.

There were cheers and someone tossed a paper cup at him.

The bowling alley felt like a strange memory to Avery already—the music, the smell of the grill, the way every person here was linked to it, playing their part as if that was all that mattered. He wanted it all put in a museum somehow, a thing that was alive in America in October 19, 1962, something that could never be again.

He went down the steps, pushed open the door and was back on the sidewalk night. It was almost quiet. He looked along the street and he could see their car. The windshield glimmered with the reflected Star Lanes sign.

Opening the passenger door, he loaded the shovel in across the backseat. What a relief to know he was done carrying that around.

He got in the front seat, sat down and shut the door.

SPACE

There wasn't much to do in the car. He was just glad to be out of the bowling alley, off the streets and away from everything going full tilt.

A few cars went past, one with chrome that flickered. An airplane flew over the city, blinking its tiny lights in a vast clouded sky. He wondered who was up in there, looking down.

After another minute of sitting there in thought, Avery reached with the key. He turned the ignition switch to the Auxiliary setting so he could play the radio. The light on the dial glowed ghostly like a handful of fireflies.

He recognized the President's voice. Who didn't know that voice?

"*—the spirit of peace and cooperation with which we approach the decades ahead. This manner of opening the fair is in keeping with the exposition's space age theme. Literally we are reaching out through space, on the new ocean, to a star which we have never seen, to intercept sound in the form of radio waves already ten thousand years old, to start the fair.*" There was a sort of tumbling river stone sound, like what you would hear if you stuck your head underwater in Padden Creek. "*The sound emanates from Cassiopeia A in the northern sky. Astronomers see only a faint filmy cloud where the entire constellation is located. How different did our globe look ten thousand years ago when that sound started its long voyage? We hope that the light which starts from that star today—ten thousand years, later arrives here—will see a happy and a peaceful world.*"

Avery switched off the radio. He saw his mother leave Star Lanes. She had her big coat on and she carried a white paper bag in one hand, her purse in the other. Way above in the sky past the *Herald* building was a break in the clouds, no bigger than a field, but you could see a few stars dropped in there.

SATURDAY, October 20, 1962

GUNSHOT

Saturday morning, it happened just after Avery buried the red heart-colored stone.

He was a little ways out in the apple field, not far from his favorite sitting tree. He had been careful to cut the grassy square of topsoil so that it could fit back over the deep hole he dug. Nobody would ever know that stone was down below.

Avery was brushing away what crumbs of soil remained, the shovel leaned against a tree trunk, when he heard the gunshot.

It wasn't that unusual a sound. Most people on farms had guns, to shoot at the things that tried to eat what you worked so hard to grow. There were deer and boys with guns; it wasn't so strange to hear the crack of a rifle. His grandfather had a gun rack in the living room with his hunting rifles in rows. But the sound was so sudden and out of the blue and so nearby that Avery jumped.

It scared a few crows off into the sky. They cawed and scattered.

Avery looked at the hill in the direction he was sure it came from and he knew something terrible had happened. The orchard was dead silent. It was like lack of atmosphere. He was back in the unworldly, like those games he used to play when he was a boy, when the fields were other planets and he was an astronaut, looking for signs of life.

Avery stood up in slow motion and took a step toward the hill. There were fences he would have to go over or around, the creeks crossed by tippy planks, the long weedy flats that used to be gardens tilled in neat rows. You used to find sweet peas, lettuce, strawberries. When he was a boy he used to walk by them as a spaceman. He took slow careful steps in the soil.

He brushed through the weeds and skirted a mound of blackberry. His feet were moving faster now, not so dreamlike and heavy. The apple trees all leaned, as if pointing towards Hickory Hill. It felt like he was the only thing moving or making a sound, running in a painting, heart pounding.

When he climbed the last fence, he could see the roof of his grandparents' house. He followed the path. His jeans and shoes were now wet from the morning dew.

TIPPED

Why did he think it might be General? For a split second he knew who it was but he told himself it was the old horse instead. That horse had been around for a hundred years. Wasn't that long enough? The pale color dropped on the ground wasn't General though. He knew that.

There was a bird chirping in the big pile of blackberry that made a wall on his right. A few others joined in, little finches, juncos.

Not far from the pond, lay his grandfather. He wore a gray coat. That's what made Avery think of General. Beside his crumpled body was one of his hunting rifles. It looked like a branch that had fallen from a tree and knocked him down. Avery wished his grandfather would get to his feet, rub his head and curse and turn and notice Avery and wave. He wished he had a stone to make that happen.

But he could tell something bad happened—that noise that cut the air and turned the world quiet put an end to the way things were.

Avery let his wet legs and wet feet take him there. It was like crossing a deep puddle. He could see more. His grandfather lay face down, not like he was sleeping though. Warren's limbs were cruelly twisted.

When he stopped, Avery could see the blood in the grass next to the old man's head. The stock of the gun shined walnut, the barrel pointed away towards the distant mountains. It didn't seem like Avery was looking at something that really happened.

"Avery!"

He jumped. Time caught up. He almost fell as he turned his body around and the land tipped like a merry-go-round.

Dallas Clay ran from the house towards him. He had his red hunting jacket on. He was the second bright red in the gray and yellowy October field. Dallas ran past Avery and stopped on his knees beside Warren. He tipped the old man over and Avery instantly looked away.

He tried to look away from a lot of what happened that day. When the police and the ambulance arrived, he tried not to see the way they put his grandfather on a stretcher, put him in and shut the door. He tried not to notice the way Dallas wiped his hands off in the cold pale weeds and how he used a bucket of hot water and bleach on that spot by the pond. His grandmother held onto the officer's arm and Avery watched her feet in those thin blue sneakers. Everyone crunched on those seashells going back and forth on the path from the house to the cars. Avery stared out the window at the trees and the sky and the telephone wires and they all got out at the hospital. It was a long horrible day, yet somehow his grandfather was still alive.

CAFETERIA

Avery's mother and grandmother were let into a room to see Warren. Avery got as far as the doorway, until he saw all the machines and hoses and a wheezing thing that breathed like a heart attached to his grandfather. There wasn't anything they could do, but the women stood near and Avery held the door frame.

When the nurse ushered them back out, they returned to a waiting room. Avery's mother put some money in his hand and said, "Why don't you go to the cafeteria?" She squeezed his hand. "I think we'll go home in an hour or so."

"Okay."

"Eileen, would you like Avery to bring you back a sandwich or something?"

"No, I'm fine." Eileen had placed herself on one of the plastic chairs. She waved a thin wrist. "You run along, dear."

He did. He followed the white hallways. He took an elevator down to the ground floor. A sign pointed the way down one more short hall and then he was in the cafeteria.

There were twenty or so people seated at tables around the big light blue room. The tall windows showed the view of bare trees and the parking lot.

There was nobody else in line. Avery got a tray and ran it along the counter that led him past the kitchen, silver vats filled with pasta, meats and vegetables and pots of soup. There was also a grill and Avery caught the eye of the cook.

"What can I get for you?"

"Hi," Avery said. "Could I get a grilled cheese sandwich?"

"You got it."

The cook went to work preparing it. Avery wondered how it would compare with the bowling alley food. Would a sandwich made in a hospital taste better?

As the cook swept the sandwich off the grill onto a plate with some fried potatoes, Avery had drifted along. He was stopped in front of the ice cream. "Can I get one of these too?"

"Of course, your highness."

There were little green bowls of Neapolitan kept cold.

The cook passed Avery a hot plate and a bowl of ice cream. "Anything else?"

"No thanks."

"Alright. You can pay at the register over there."

Avery carried his tray, paid and got some change from the old lady. Then it was the cafeteria waiting for him. Where would he go?

ICE CREAM

They were mostly old people in the room. There was a guy with a broken arm trying to cut his food. There was also a girl his age, busy reading a book.

When he sat down at the table across from her, she looked up at him and they both smiled, but Avery looked quickly back to his tray. Still shy, he told himself. He stared at his potatoes. What a dunce. He forgot the ketchup.

He left his tray and walked back to where the register shared the counter with a rack full of ketchup bottles and napkins, forks and spoons. He got everything he needed.

When he turned, he noticed the girl had moved across to his table. He walked back slowly. She read from her book as if she had been there all along.

Then she caught his eye. "Hello."

Avery said, "Hello."

"Are you the Emperor of Ice Cream?" She pointed at the bowl on his tray.

"Oh," he said. "I know that...Where's that from?"

She tipped her thick book up from the table so Avery could see the starry cover, the picture of the author and the title.

"Wallace Stevens! I knew that." He sat down and set the ketchup bottle by his tray. "I have a book with some of his poems in it. I usually have it with me. You were smart to bring a book here."

"We come here a lot. My family is very accident prone."

The way she said it made Avery laugh. He thought of them like a silent film family, hanging onto clocks, swinging over waterfalls, walking on tightropes, falling walls.

"We are! Guess what we're here for this time."

"Was someone hit by lightning?" He took a bite of his sandwich.

"That was last summer. This time, my little brother made wings and tried to fly off the roof."

Avery swallowed. "I always wanted to try that."

"Well don't!" she laughed. It was a great laugh. "What are you here for?"

His smile faded. He looked at his food. The sandwich was getting cold; the ice cream was starting to melt. He waited for the moment to pass. "Would you like my ice cream?"

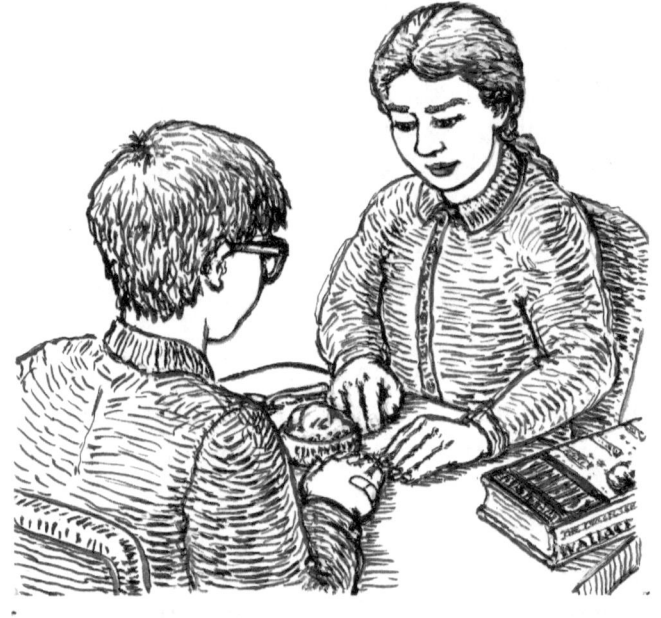

She reached out, "Thank you."

"I don't know why I got it." He pushed the bowl to her, gave her a spoon and grinned, "I must have had a feeling you would want it."

She took a bite and closed her eyes. "Delicious."

He smiled. He was starting to like her. Or maybe he did from the moment he saw her, like people do in poetry.

SOON

"I don't know if it's true or not," she said, "but anytime something bad happens, I like to think something good will happen soon."

He almost told her about his grandfather. He almost told her that his grandfather had been sick and there was no way he would ever get well and knowing that, the old man had gone out into the field behind his house with a gun. And they knew it was probably no accident. The night before, Warren called Dallas Clay, who had seen such terrible things in the war, to come to the farm, to the pond in the morning. Only Avery heard the shot first and got there before Dallas. And now his grandfather was upstairs, somehow barely still alive and if anything good could follow that, Avery would like to know how?

She reached across the tray and touched his hand. She ran a finger over the band-aids.

SUNDAY, October 21, 1962

PRACTICE

The Sunday morning *Herald* had a photo of the President on the front page. Kennedy looked like he was in a hurry, putting on a raincoat. He was trying to smile. He wore a black hat and a black suit. *Kennedy Cancels Visit. On Advice of his physician, the Chief Executive canceled the remainder of his weekend trip due to a slight cold.* There was more to the story below. *Kennedy Calls Off His Trip to Seattle.*

Avery thought of Robert Canfield.

He pushed the newspaper away, across the table. They wouldn't be at the hospital for long. He waited in the cafeteria. This time he had his big book of poetry, but he didn't feel like reading. He was looking for the girl from yesterday. It was about the same time of day.

Where was she?

He didn't even know who she was. He needed so much practice. It all happened so fast. He was so surprised when they said their goodbyes, he forgot to ask for her name.

When she had to leave, he said, "Sorry I didn't remember it was Wallace Stevens."

She said, "That's alright, I knew you knew." Before she left the cafeteria she took a book from the bag on her shoulder. She said, "Here," and she gave him a book by E.E. Cummings. A present from a girl...

And before he could ask for her name or anything that might bring them back together again, she was gone.

Without her, the cafeteria was a big cold ice-skating rink.

COURAGE

Before they got to the mortuary, Avery asked if he could get out of the car. Truthfully, he wasn't much of a hero. He didn't like danger or death. "I can walk home from here," he told his mother.

"We're almost there. Have some courage. She slowed and stopped the car at a red traffic light. She and Eileen beside her had been quiet all the way from the hospital. "At least come with us there and then you can leave."

Avery watched the street pick up speed again. All the grains in the pavement blurred like the current in a stream.

The radio was on, tuned to his grandmother's station, and a song began that Avery knew she would know was a sign. Anytime it played on the radio when Avery was over having tea and talking, she would stop. If Warren was at the table, he would get quiet too, watching out the window as if he could see them not long ago in a lost age. They never said that was their song, but it was clear that "Moonlight in Vermont" meant something to them. And hearing it on the car radio at that moment, it was like Warren's spirit had stopped on its way to somewhere else just long enough to hover about the tall radio station tower and scatter that song into the sky in search of them.

The song took them to the mortuary parking lot where it ended when the car engine rattled off. It felt as if a jukebox had played its nickel and now it sat in a quiet shadowed corner again.

Avery got out of the car. A cold breeze made his torn coat sleeve flutter. He regarded the gray stone windowless building. It looked like a screen from a Count Misfit movie. He had the feeling Bela Lugosi was in there sharpening his fangs.

Avery hung his arms over the car doorframe and

when his mother got out of the car and shut her door, Avery groaned, "Uhhh..."

"Just help your grandmother out," she said. "Then you can go."

He opened Eileen's door and took her hand.

She seemed to float out; he felt like he was holding onto a paper version of his grandmother. She could have been folded origami. If the breeze was any stronger, she might be swept into the sky. "I'm okay now, dear. You can run along. We'll see you at home."

"It looks like it might rain, Avery," his mother said. "You can stay in the car and wait for us."

"No thanks." He wasn't about to sit in a morgue parking lot. He had witnessed too many movies and late night radio shows to do that. Wasn't it only last week he scooted through Bayview Cemetery at night with a bonfired car and the police at his heels? How far could he push his luck? Weren't all his adventures leading him here?

He watched them disappear. When the door shut, he squeezed his hands tight and hoped they would come back out again...Of course they would, he told himself. It was his grandfather whose journey was ending in there. He would be turned into ashes and the ashes would be poured into the sea. From then on, he would live on as memory, and sometimes reappear in a dream.

Avery would come to terms with it, but it would take walking and time.

RAIN

So he walked away from the mortuary parking lot with its garden plots cut low for winter and he turned at the hedgerows and followed the sidewalk as it paralleled the bay. There were some kids in a front yard and Avery wondered how it would be living this close to death. They seemed used to it. He watched two crows chase a seagull across the road. They shot up over a fence and a roof, around a TV antenna.

Two blocks later he felt the first drop of rain. He wiped it off his face and looked at the wet to see if it was made of the same dark charcoal as the clouds. He wouldn't have been surprised. He was prepared to turn statue-colored by that gray October rain.

A few water dots appeared on his tattered coat sleeve. Three beads on his glasses lenses. But he was sure he could get to Robert Canfield's before the rain set in.

Down the last hill, Avery caught a glimpse of the bay. There were whitecaps and one small sailboat making for land.

The wind kicked some leaves ahead of him and they scratched off the curb into the street with him as he crossed. He could have been taking them for a walk. He saw the apartment where Tony's father lived, a stuccoed wall with windows, and he hoped Tony wasn't looking out.

Avery left his leaves behind as he hopped up the curb. Robert Canfield's house was in front of him. Avery hurried past the mailbox, up the cracked cement pathway and knocked on the door. The big window was half curtained, but there was a light on inside. He pressed the doorbell too, just in case. The rain began to patter on the street behind him. In another second it turned to a hiss. If he stepped back into it, he would be soaked.

The door opened with a click and squeak and Robert Canfield stood there surprised. "Avery!"

"I wasted my wishing stone and now my grandfather is dead."

MAYBE

Robert Canfield had a library of poetry. Books filled two walls of the room from floor to ceiling. When he returned from the kitchen with two cups and a teapot, Avery was sitting in the chair by the window holding a book.

Robert set a cup on the table next to Avery and took a seat on a big chair in the corner. "You were lucky to get here before that rain."

The window was made of submarine glass. The house was towed below the ocean; the trees waved like seaweed and the birds looked for shelter like fish.

Robert said, "You know, I haven't always had the best of luck with the stones either. There have been people I wished I could have done more for. Sometimes other forces are at play. Look how it is with the Kennedys. I thought I had them safe and sound." He tapped the newspaper on the armrest. "And now I read the President won't be returning to the area."

"I saw that too. What are you going to do?"

"Start all over of course. Who knows when they'll be back this way?"

"Maybe never," Avery said suddenly.

Robert nodded. "Maybe."

"What are we supposed to do now? Me and my mom and my grandmother? Didn't he think about what it would be like for us without him? What kind of world do we have now?"

"A new one," Robert said. He finished the tea in his cup and held it empty for a moment. Robert liked classical music and the big old wooden radio dial glowed with it.

"Well," Avery said. "I made a terrible mistake with that stone. I was selfish. I don't know why I didn't use it for my grandfather. Maybe I could have saved his life."

"Maybe." Robert refilled his tea and agreed, "Maybe, maybe, maybe..." He said each maybe slow as a paddlewheel. He took another drink.

"Is this tea from Japan?" Avery asked.

"China."

"It's different than the kind my grandmother makes. She likes the English kind that comes in teabags."

"That's from India." Robert held his cup with both hands wrapped around. There wasn't much left, mostly steam.

Avery put the book down and had some of his tea. All of a sudden he was tasting China, the flowers from the ground around a mountainside, the same cold mountain where poetry sprung from cracks in the rock, where a fog crept across the land and dug its heels into the planted rows cultivated for hundreds of years and he followed the taste on the long journey it took across the Pacific Ocean to fill his cup. When he opened his eyes, he returned to the room, the rainy window, the walls of books and the painted scroll of a crane flying over impossible looking rounded, treed hills.

"Even though it's too late, I'd like to find a stone for my grandfather."

"Sure," Robert said. "We can go to Poe's Point. That's a good place to look. I might even find some new Kennedy stones, so I'll be ready for their next visit."

"Do you want to go tomorrow?"

"Okay."

"Can I meet you there after school?"

"That sounds good." Robert stood up. "In the meantime, you should telephone your mother in case she's home wondering where you are. You can tell her I'll drive you back. There's the phone."

Robert left Avery to make his call and brought his

cup to the kitchen. The latest Kennedy news had been taped to the refrigerator that morning. He paused and looked at the photo of the troubled president who hurried into his raincoat to get back to the east coast. *Fair officials were disappointed when Kennedy had to fly home from Chicago because of a cold.*

"Alright, Mr. Kennedy...If you say so..." Robert set his cup on the counter. Rain ran across the window.

He walked over to the wall and looked at the old photograph. It showed the familiar island out in the bay on a sunny day some years ago. A little sailboat floated in the distance. Sometimes it would float close on the current with a sail full of wind, sometimes it would drift with the tide. At night, when the Moon shined on the water, it might pull ashore or drop anchor in a cove. He knew what it meant to want to keep people safe from the dangers of the world. He had been doing it for years.

THE WORLD'S SMALLEST ISLAND

Robert walked back to the other room as Avery was hanging up the phone.

"They're still not home," he told Robert.

"I'm not surprised. All the arrangements that have to be done..." Robert put his raincoat on. "They'll be in need of your help, Avery."

"I know." Avery stared out the window.

"Well, let's get you back. You feel better?"

Avery nodded. The tea had helped. And knowing tomorrow they would find another stone helped too. He followed Robert out the squeaky door into the rain.

"I hope it's not raining like this tomorrow," Robert said. There was a cement walk around the side of the driveway. "Then again, all the rain will make the beach rocks shine. It might make it easier to find what we're looking for."

Avery didn't know that much about cars but he knew Robert's was pretty old, 1940s he guessed. You still saw them once in a while. They had a different air to them, nothing like the cars of the 1950s, or now, with silver chrome and streamlining and comfort. Robert's car looked like a hermit crab hunched in the rain.

"It's a 1942 Plymouth," Robert said as he opened the door for Avery. The big door squeaked as much as going in the house.

Avery liked all the silver metal and knobs and vents on the dashboard. Sitting on the thick red cushion facing the split windshield, it was like waiting for a movie to begin in front of him—a movie with gangsters, spies, the Bowery and docks in the fog.

When Robert got in behind the wheel, Avery said, "This is the car you take to the Drive-In?"

"I've been going there since it opened in 1955,"

Robert laughed. "I also like pictures in the theater, but there's something extra special about seeing a movie in the outdoors. You have to enjoy these little miracles while you can." He turned the key and the car gnashed its teeth. "Sometimes it won't start the first time." He tried again and the engine gave a cough and a ragged buzz. "There we go," he said, revving the motor. He put his arm on the seat and looked behind him. The Plymouth whirred into reverse down the driveway and bounced onto the stream the street had become.

"Look at all that water," Robert said. He started the window wipers and they tiredly flicked at the soaked glass.

All the water reminded Avery of the pond. His grandfather let him pretend it was an ocean and he pointed out a little speck of green in the middle of all the water. He told Avery it was The World's Smallest Island. This miniature Hawaii appeared overnight, he told Avery. He said Avery should swim out to it and see if there were coral reefs, white beaches, microscopic palm trees and a living volcano peak. And Avery ran inside and put on swim trunks and came running back to his grandfather, waiting by the cattails. Then Avery stepped into the smooth, muddy shallows. When it got deeper, Avery pushed himself forward and he was floating, swimming. It was a hot sunny summer day years ago. Avery didn't have to get there to see it wasn't an island. It rollicked from the waves he made swimming. But he kept going all the way until he could tread water in place and touch the edge of the green maple leaf. Using his imagination, he could see it was The World's Smallest Island. There really were coral reefs, white beaches, palm trees and a steaming volcano. That's what his grandfather wanted him to see. Avery left it stationed there and paddled back to shore until his toes could press into that soft mud. His grandfather was leaning out over the cattail, holding out his hand. He had his soft plaid workshirt off and when he pulled Avery onto land, he wrapped the warm shirt around the boy.

The wiper blades made oar-like passes at the rain.

Avery told Robert he lived on Donovan, up near the Rock. That's all the direction anyone needed in those days.

MONDAY, October 22, 1962

KNOWING

There was no way of knowing Monday, October 22 in 1962 would be an historic day. It began like nearly every other school morning, the clock saying get up, the bed being so warm, with sleep saying it was so much better to stay. Avery turned the alarm off and made himself sit up. Could he hear a faint brush of rain on the roof? Would he be standing in that, out at the bus stop? He hoped not. His room in the eaves was all gray and blue.

He thought about his talk with Robert Canfield. He seemed to remember a conversation with Perry Roberts, but it may have been a dream. He thought about the frogs around the little dark pond, the purple sky and stars and his grandfather sat beside him in his rocking chair. He took out his first and last cigarette for the day. After a while, Avery knew, the ghosts will fade away.

Avery was about to move out of bed when he heard the floor creaking downstairs and footsteps on the stairs.

His mother appeared. "Good morning, Avery. I was wondering if you would like to stay home from school today? We have a lot of work to help out Grandma."

After a yawn, Avery said, "Okay."

"I made us a big breakfast. I'll go call the school." She went down the stairs then he could hear her in the hall. Further off, he could hear the kitchen radio.

Avery thought about laying back down. How long would it take to fall asleep again? A minute? Less? In the gloom, he noticed the three books on his bedside table: three books of poetry... The start of his collection. *Tulips & Chimneys*, the present from the girl in the hospital stood at the end closest to him. Maybe he could find a stone for her today too? Everything felt easier with her though; it didn't seem like he needed to wish desperately for her. They already knew each other and would be floating back again, he just knew it. Still, he hoped it would be soon.

He got dressed and went down the stairs and for breakfast he even had half a cup of coffee. Then his mother drove them to Hickory. They left the car parked by the anchor. A jay shrieked and flew down the hill telling all the other birds they were there.

It already felt strange, like something you were used to seeing had been taken out of a painting. Where's the windmill? Where's the lighthouse? Didn't there used to be a boat there?

The brass bell was still there by the door, but for the first time since before he was tiptoe tall enough to reach that string, Avery didn't want to ring it. He stood on the broken shells while his mother knocked on the door.

As she pulled it open, she called, "Hello, Eileen?" It seemed too quiet inside. She let herself inside. "Hello?"

Avery stayed on the doorstep. He didn't want to go in the house if there was another bad surprise.

"He didn't want anyone else to find him that way," Dallas told Avery two days ago at the hospital. But Avery heard the gunshot and discovered the gray shape in the weeds first.

"Eileen?" his mother said. "There you are!" He could hear them through the screen door. They were probably in the kitchen. His grandmother may have been in the bedroom. There was a lot to put away.

Without knowing, Avery backed off the doorstep. All the birds left the tree feeder in a flurry. He took the path, some of it laid with flat stones, and walked alongside the house past the bright kitchen windows and the horseshoe nailed to the corner, old and rusted and turned to hold luck. His feet and cuffs were getting damp from the dew, on his way towards the pond.

WINDBLOWN

It wasn't quite raining, but there was a gray cold on everything. Out in the clearing away from the house and trees, the sky hung thoughtless and uncolored above the pond.

It was quiet. Avery's shoes made all the noise.

He looked at the pond now appearing. There were tall bent broken swords of cattails along its edge. His grandfather would have been waiting for the redwing blackbirds to show up.

Avery didn't go to the exact spot where his grandfather was shot. He wasn't here for that. He stood on the little rise of hill and observed the pond.

He didn't even know there was a wind. The pond showed it. The nickel surface fanned and rippled with the hands of a breeze smoothing across it. There were more than a few leaf islands dotted about the water. They were all on the move, some of them bumping into each other. Avery stood on the knoll and watched them.

A low flying crow passed over the pond and Avery followed its black reflection. He decided to sit down and as he did, he remembered that famous haiku by Basho about the frog noise in the pond. It must have been months since any frog tried to jump in this cold water. And now his grandfather was a memory.

Life had changed. This place was different. Avery knew it wasn't just his grandfather that was gone. He had a feeling it was only a matter of time before this farm would be gone and then the orchard and the other family farms too. He picked up a fallen leaf. The cold wet of the ground was seeping into him so Avery stood up.

He walked down to the pond where the ground was soft and he stretched his hand and tossed the leaf out. It fluttered, then glided like a bird. Where it stuck to the water was a new island on the map. Time moved it slowly from shore to join the other leaves further out.

"Avery!"

His mother was calling him from the house.

He looked in that direction. He didn't want to yell back. It was peaceful and he wasn't far. He could see the rooftop and the trees. A couple of tall firs waved their thick branches.

When he turned around to look at the pond, his leaf, whichever one it was, had become a part of the wind-blown pond.

LEGEND

He wasn't surprised to find out. Wasn't it just what he was thinking about at the pond? His grandmother didn't want to live in the house alone. She didn't want to be on a farm anymore. She wanted to live in town, in an apartment, where there were other people around.

Avery looked at his teacup and watched what happened as he poured milk in. All of a sudden, clouds formed in his cup. The rust color world stormed with them. He dipped his spoon in and slowly spun the end until the tea was filled with a constant gray like the sky today.

His grandmother didn't even have the radio on. Those songs were a part of it too. She wanted a whole new life. As she packed, she told them about her mother coming from Scotland bringing only what she could carry in a big steamer trunk. That's what she wanted to do, she said. She was leaving this place for another shore.

His mother listened with a growing alarm. She would say things to try and bring Eileen back, but it wasn't working and gradually she knew.

They had a big job ahead of them. They would have to dismantle everything that had been here for years. It was all going, pulled down like the stage of a play.

Avery was sent to the shop, the tool shed out behind the house. His grandmother said to take out whatever he wanted to keep.

When he opened the screen door, the birds scattered from their feeders. He wondered what would happen to them? There had been birds on that tree since Avery was a baby. They were like family. Was his grandmother going to pack them in that steamer trunk, between folded linen and clothes and photo albums? No. They would probably drift off into the leaves. Maybe some of their songs would tell of all the years they spent here. If their songs were like poetry, their life on Hickory Hill would be remembered as a bird legend.

Avery opened the rusted latch on the shed. The room smelled of oil and sawdust. It was a room where his grandfather had worked on his projects—boats, wooden shelves, flowerboxes and reading lamps. Tulips and chimneys, Avery thought, looking around. It was Warren's poetry remains Avery found—that half-finished sailboat hull was the thing he took in his hands. On the walls and benches were all the tools. Saws with worn handles and sharp silver teeth, a C-shaped drill with a round handle shiny as a chestnut. He couldn't bring himself to take anything, just that sailboat shaped block of wood. He wished he could close the door of the shed and everything in it would disappear to be with his grandfather.

He turned the rusted latch into its groove and carried the unfinished boat back to the house. On the doorstep, he almost rang the bell. It was instinct. The rope that hung from it was attached to his grandfather. If he heard it now, where would he be and would he want to come back? Could he return like Gizmo, one last time? Anyway, Avery knew that bell's tone—he could hear it in his head—he didn't have to pull the string to recall everything the way it was.

SECRETS

In the afternoon, Avery left the house. He left rooms that he had known all his life, raked into piles and put in boxes. He didn't know how they could do it. After a long day of it, he told them he needed to take a walk.

With deep breaths of that apple air, he hurried up the crackling path, past where the irises grew in the summer, the mailbox and anchor, and he was on the gravel road that rolled atop the hill to join with Donovan. He went the other direction though.

School would be out soon. Avery mapped his way along yards and shortcuts, and chose a side street, so the school buses wouldn't see him. He didn't want to be seen by everyone going home from a long day of classes.

He passed a row of chicken houses. They clucked and steamed like wooden boats. He was used to the smell, but he was glad he grew up in an orchard.

McKenzie slanted down towards the bay. It was a big gray mirror of the sky. He saw the island, dark black green, and asleep as a dog. He walked along the sidewalk, every so often kicking some leaves, noticing the houses that were decorated for Halloween. Pumpkins on porch ledges carved with faces that watched him back. One house had a skeleton in a rocking chair. Soon this street would be a nighttime of little ghouls in costumes running door to door.

He unzipped his coat pocket and took out an apple. Living in an apple orchard, you might think he would tire of apples. Not so. This time of year he would have two or three a day. Not to mention a cool glass of cider from the refrigerator anytime he was thirsty.

He ate the apple while he walked.

The road flattened for a while then dropped again and Avery crossed to Harris Ave, a straight shot to the sea. He could see the tin roofs of the cannery, the cranes at the shipyard and the tall chimneys billowing smoke. If he was a bowling ball, he could roll thundering fast past all the windows and doors, trees and telephone poles, and if he didn't strike a car or pop up over the curb, he could fly right off the clacking wooden pier at the end. And if he could hold a prayer like one of those wishing stones, he would remain unfound in the harbor under a hundred feet of water, silt and kelp. Alone forever, he would know the secrets of the deep like that lobster in his poetry book.

FUTURISTIC

He stopped at the corner and waited for the traffic light to change.

On the edge of the sidewalk next to the gas station lot stood a telephone booth. With its glass sides and position right there next to the flow of traffic, it resembled one of those gondolas from the Seattle World's Fair. Avery wished he could get in, shut the door and be pulled into the air on wires. Up there, he could look at the town—the misty hills, islands and bay. He would wave to Bobby Burns the chimney sweep, and all the people who walked along. He would float by at seagull height, looking out on the unfinished roofs and green weedy streets as the glass contraption soared to the last bit of land. Then he would get out right where he wanted to be.

Avery thought about his town, all connected by floating transportation as he walked by the pharmacy, the television repair and the hardware store and saloons and the boarded up brick buildings. Avery hadn't been to the World's Fair. He heard lots of stories at school about the Space Needle, the Monorail, the Space Whirl, the actual Mercury capsule housed there, the islands of Hawaii exhibit, the Food Circus, the Bubbleator, the water fountain that changed its flow, the Flight to Mars ride and the bumper cars. Why not have a fun, futuristic world right here in their town? Why wasn't it possible?

By then he was into the flats where it hadn't been built on and there were ragged fields on either side. All the trees were gone, used up long ago for settlers' houses or firewood. The battered road led over the drained inlet by the wharves where it was low tide, muddy, and a few seagulls hunched along scavenging. He thought of it as another side of the planet. The sulfurous atmosphere was heavy with the din of machinery, not unlike all the highway construction at the polar extreme of Donovan. Was the future just about who could make the most noise? Hydrogen bombs, Atlas rockets, roads that never stopped being made...

A truck crawled out of the Plywood Company lot on his right and Avery was washed in the exhaust as it coughed into gears. There were boats and ships up on blocks, in dry dock, above the screech and sparks of welders. The Pacific American Fisheries Cannery stood in rust and old paint along the water in front of him as he turned left at the Forge Company's big walls. You could show a movie on that corrugated siding. There was a big dent pushed out from inside. Avery guessed why. It sounded like a dragon lived in there, breathing fire and bristling its iron scales.

There was no sidewalk. He followed a gravel road, just a few parked cars, a tree, and further along until he saw Robert's Plymouth.

GOOD NIGHT

Poe's Point with its backdrop of islands, boats and sweep of the bay was a beautiful spot on a sunny day. This late Monday afternoon the waves showed some white teeth and the clouds clenched and it looked like rain was on the way.

Avery could see Robert reading the newspaper held up against the windshield. Hopefully he had not been there too long.

Avery stopped alongside the passenger side and rapped on the window.

Robert waved and put the paper down on the seat.

"Hey, Avery," he said as he got out of the car and shut the door. "How was school?"

"Actually, I didn't go. I was helping at my grandmother's house all day."

"How is she doing?"

"She wants to move." As they walked towards the shore, Avery told him how the day went. Everything was going into boxes. The house would be emptied and put up for sale. It was like his grandmother was in a wind that was picking her up and taking her away. "Maybe I should find a stone for her. I think she needs one more than anyone."

They left the grass and their shoes slid into the beach stones and sand. There was a thick tangled line of seaweed washed ashore, left like yarn at the tidemark. Avery saw clam shells and blue mussels. His grandmother would have brought a shopping bag to fill. But she wouldn't need shells at an apartment.

Robert agreed. He stopped walking and said, "There seems to be a lot of those stones around here. You can feel them, can't you?"

Avery took a step away from him. He scanned the

jumble of broken shells, bits of wood and weed, the flotsam of shipwrecks and the junk thrown out at sea.

Robert was right. Avery could feel the stones. Some of them hummed to him. As he walked they called out, shifting beneath his feet. He just had to find the right one for his grandmother. It was another talent like dowsing and poetry. And it came to him naturally.

He reached down and his fingers went around the smooth round shape of a blue stone with white cloudy marbling. He cupped both hands about it and held it like an egg. It was the right one.

When he turned around, Robert held up his arm and waved. Avery carried the stone towards land.

"You found it," Robert said.

Avery nodded.

They stood there staying quiet. Robert watched the sea. Avery could see the rain sweeping over the top of the Chuckanut Hills, a mile away in the air.

"I guess you're ready to go home now. I feel rain." Robert crunched the stones. "I'll give you a ride."

Avery was already thinking of his grandmother. He turned the stone in his hand as he wished for her.

If the car radio was on, they would hear the speech just beginning. It was on all the stations across America.

Good evening, my fellow citizens.

When they got in the Plymouth, Robert knew Avery wanted to be quiet with his thoughts. He made sure the radio was off when he started the car.

But there was a radio in the office at the Forge Company and it was on. People in there left their stations to listen.

Within the past week unmistakable evidence has established the fact that a series of offensive missile sites is now in preparation on that imprisoned island. The purposes of these bases can be none other than to provide a nuclear strike capability against the Western Hemisphere.

The old car passed that dented dragon's cave and drove through the signals driven in the air, transmitted from the big antenna at Channel 12.

A television was on in the break room at the Cannery.

Our own strategic missiles have never been transferred to the territory of any other nation under a cloak of secrecy and deception.

Robert turned on Harris toward the hill, just the sound of the engine.

We have no desire to dominate or conquer any other nation or impose our system upon its people.

President Kennedy glowed in the row of black and white TVs in the window of Coast To Coast Television and Radio Repair, but neither Robert or Avery was aware.

Our policy has been one of patience and restraint, as befits a peaceful and powerful nation, which leads a worldwide alliance. We have been determined not to be diverted from our central concerns by mere irritants and fanatics. But now further action is required—and it is underway; and these actions may only be the beginning. We will not prematurely or unnecessarily risk the costs of worldwide nuclear war in which even the fruits of victory would be ashes in our mouth—but neither will we shrink from that risk at any time it must be faced.

Robert turned right and they drove along the row of trees in a wood turning dark for the night. Past the IGA grocery and Gull gas station, onto Donovan, they passed houses with their lights turned on and TV glows and their radios on windowsills, in living rooms and kitchens.

We have in the past made strenuous efforts to limit the spread of nuclear weapons. We have proposed the elimination of all arms and military bases in a fair and effective disarmament treaty. We are prepared to discuss new proposals for the removal of tensions on both sides—including the possibilities of a genuinely independent Cuba, free to determine its own destiny. We have no wish to war with the Soviet Union, for we are a peaceful people who desire to live in peace with all other peoples.

The Plymouth windshield was now dotted with rain. The engine groaned as the hill began again.

Avery held that rock then he sighed and said, "I think I'll get out at my grandmother's house." He pointed at the street coming up. "You can stop on Hickory."

"Okay." Robert steered left onto the gravel road.

"This is good," said Avery as they stopped at the anchor. "Thanks." He put a hand on the door. "I'm sorry about wasting my other wish."

"I'm sure it wasn't wasted."

"I wished on a girl I don't even know."

Robert smiled. "That's alright, Avery. You have a big heart."

Avery opened the door. He stepped outside.

The air was charged with the electricity of television, radio, autumn leaves falling down with cold rain. Avery waved the clenched hand holding the stone and he shut the heavy door with a clang.

My fellow citizens...

The words floated silently, unseen around him, blanketing the town and all of listening America.

Let no one doubt that this is a difficult and dangerous effort on which we have set out. No one can foresee precisely what course it will take or what costs or casualties will be incurred. Many months of sacrifice and self-discipline lie ahead—months in which both our patience and our will will be tested, months in which many threats and denunciations will keep us aware of our dangers. But the greatest danger of all would be to do nothing.

But Avery didn't follow the path to his grandmother's house.

Robert's car backed out onto Donovan and Avery waved farewell to those red lights leaving.

There was somewhere else Avery wanted to go.

The path we have chosen for the present is full of hazards, as all paths are; but it is the one most consistent with our character and courage as a nation and our commitments around the world. The cost of freedom is always high-but Americans have always paid it. And one path we shall never choose, and that is the path of surrender or submission.

Along the gravel edge of Hickory, where it met with the steep shoulder of Donovan, sloped down into the weeds and brambles and the irrigation creek, it was like walking on the side of a mountain. There were some floating leaves that were blood red. He looked for that salmon as he always did, and still didn't see it.

There were other stones buried in the mud and grass and he hoped he wasn't disturbing someone else's wish. It was getting dark. The little farm creek rippled and sang. It would be added to by a night of rain and it would rise maybe another inch or so by morning.

He found a spot he liked. The stream ran over bent-over green leaves of grass. Avery pushed his hand into the icy water and combed the weeds aside. The soil was easy to dig into. A cloud formed around his hand.

Our goal is not the victory of might but the vindication of right—not peace at the expense of freedom, but both peace and freedom, here in this Hemisphere and, we hope, around the world. God willing, that goal will be achieved.

Avery put the wishing stone underwater, under the grass, safe in the flow.

Thank you and good night.

KENNEDY
by Allen Frost
January 26, 2015 6:39 AM—May 16, 2015 12:50 PM

Books by Good Deed Rain

Saint Lemonade, Allen Frost, 2014. Two novels illustrated by the author in the manner of the old Big Little Books.

Playground, Allen Frost, 2014. Poems collected from seven years of chapbooks.

Roosevelt, Allen Frost, 2015. A Pacific Northwest novel set in July, 1942, when a boy and a girl search for a missing elephant. Illustrated throughout by Fred Sodt.

5 Novels, Allen Frost, 2015. Novels written over five years, featuring circus giants, clockwork animals, detectives and time travelers.

The Sylvan Moore Show, Allen Frost, 2015. A short story omnibus of 193 stories written over 30 years.

Town in a Cloud, Allen Frost, 2015. A three-part book of poetry, written during the Bellingham rainy seasons of fall, winter, and spring.

A Flutter of Birds Passing Through Heaven: A Tribute to Robert Sund. 2016. Edited by Allen Frost and Paul Piper. The story of a legendary Ish River poet & artist.

At the Edge of America, Allen Frost, 2016. Two novels in one book blend time travel in a mythical poetic America.

Lake Erie Submarine, Allen Frost, 2016. A two week vacation in Ohio inspired these poems, illustrated by the author.

and Light, Paul Piper, 2016. Poetry written over three years. Illustrated with watercolors by Penny Piper.

The Book of Ticks, Allen Frost, 2017. A giant collection of 8 mysterious adventures featuring Phil Ticks. Illustrated throughout by Aaron Gunderson.

I Can Only Imagine, Allen Frost, 2017. Five adventures of love and heartbreak dreamed in an imaginary world. Cover & color illustrations by Annabelle Barrett.

The Orphanage of Abandoned Teenagers, Allen Frost, 2017. A fictional guide for teens and their parents. Illustrated by the author.

In the Valley of Mystic Light: An Oral History of the Skagit Valley Arts Scene, 2017. Edited by Claire Swedberg & Rita Hupy.

Different Planet, Allen Frost, 2017. Four science fiction adventures: reincarnation, robots, talking animals, outer space and clones. Cover & illustrations by Laura Vasyutynska.

Go with the Flow: A Tribute to Clyde Sanborn. 2018. Edited by Allen Frost. The life and art of a timeless river poet.

Homeless Sutra, Allen Frost, 2018. Four stories: Sylvan Moore, a flying monk, a water salesman, and a guardian rabbit.

The Lake Walker, Allen Frost 2018. A little novel set in black and white like one of those old European movies about death and life.

A Hundred Dreams Ago, Allen Frost, 2018. A winter book of poetry and prose. Cover and illustrations by Aaron Gunderson.

Almost Animals, Allen Frost, 2018. A collection of linked stories, thinking about what makes us animals.

The Robotic Age, Allen Frost, 2018. A vaudeville magician and his robot companion track down ghosts. Illustrated throughout by Aaron Gunderson.

Kennedy, Allen Frost, 2018. This sequel to *Roosevelt* is a coming-of-age fable set during two weeks in 1962, in a mythical Kennedy-land. Illustrated throughout by Fred Sodt.

find Roosevelt!

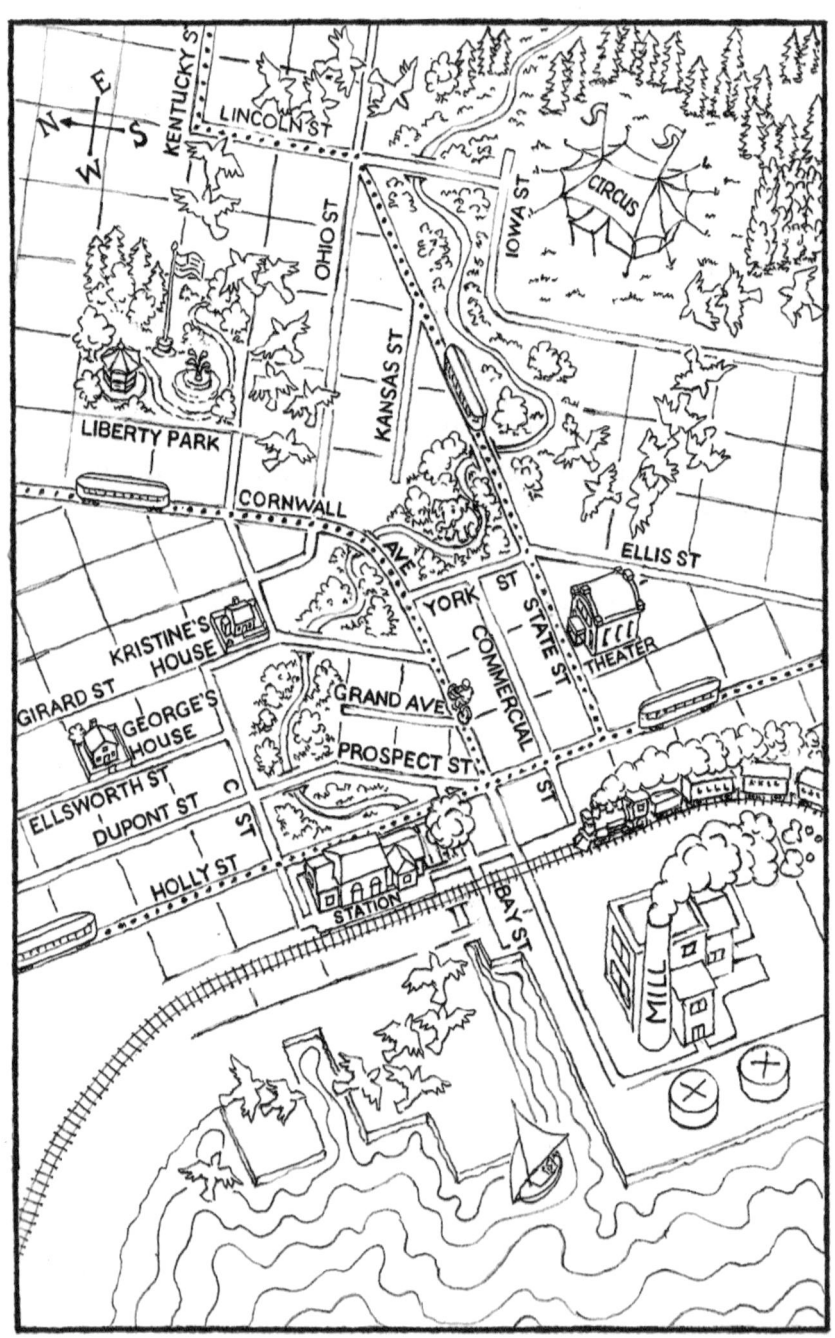

Kennedy is the sequel to *Roosevelt*, which is set 20 years previously in the same town. This is praise for *Roosevelt* :

In this novel for middle-grade readers, a Pacific Northwestern boy searches for an escaped circus elephant with help from his eccentric uncle and a friend.

It's 1942 in Bellingham, Washington, and the circus is coming to town. At the fairground, fourth-grader George is dazzled by the lights, noise, and excitement—"every sense was boiling, a million times over." Even so, George "wondered how it would be for an animal," like Roosevelt the elephant. That night, he dreams of Roosevelt escaping and finds that it's true when he returns to the now-empty circus fairground. A circus clown left behind to search for Roosevelt (who has a habit of getting loose) gives George an elephant calling horn so he can look. Meanwhile, George's brother Andrew has just been called up to the Army, and the town makes homefront preparations. With his friend Kristine and some supernatural aid from his uncle Robert, George helps Roosevelt, while Andrew makes his own escape. With his fine, poetic imagery, Frost (*5 Novels*, 2015, etc.) captures the magic not just of the circus, but of friendship, animals, summer days, and special moments: "The clicking clacking of the railroad tracks sewed up the night"; "music, laughter and voices linked together like a paperclip chain tied from house to house." Characterization is deft and effective, as when George notices an aphid on Kristine's arm and likes "the way she noticed it too and put her fingertip near it, and let it climb on so she could give it a big leaf to live on." Though Uncle Robert's magical solution is too easy, he's an interesting figure, with his top hat and daytime moviegoing. Frost also ably brings in historical details, as when a showoff kid skids his bike wheels and George isn't impressed: "Everyone knew you weren't supposed to waste rubber."

Delightful, with appealing characters and a serious edge.
—*Kirkus Review*

www.ingramcontent.com/pod-product-compliance
Lightning Source LLC
LaVergne TN
LVHW041627060526
838200LV00040B/1466